JARED DETTER

Dreams and Curses

First published by Skellig Press 2024

Copyright © 2024 by Jared Detter

All rights reserved. No part of this publication may be reproduced, stored or transmitted in any form or by any means, electronic, mechanical, photocopying, recording, scanning, or otherwise without written permission from the publisher. It is illegal to copy this book, post it to a website, or distribute it by any other means without permission.

This novel is entirely a work of fiction. The names, characters and incidents portrayed in it are the work of the author's imagination. Any resemblance to actual persons, living or dead, events or localities is entirely coincidental.

Jared Detter asserts the moral right to be identified as the author of this work.

First edition

ISBN: 979-8-9873655-5-7

This book was professionally typeset on Reedsy.
Find out more at reedsy.com

This book is dedicated to my middle son, Justus.

You've always been quick with a smile that lights up your face. I hope life continues to give you plenty of reasons to smile and that this book is one of them. Never forget that I'm proud of you.

If I find in myself a desire which no experience
in this world can satisfy, the most probable
explanation is that I was made for another
world.

C.S. LEWIS

Preface

When I was a child, my mother had the great idea of writing a birthday letter to each of her children each year that would encapsulate the major milestones and events from the previous year. She would include many funny anecdotes and things that she wanted to preserve for posterity, such as what sports I played, who my friends were, and what I most enjoyed. When we left the house, we were given 18 unopened birthday letters that we could read through. It was really quite amazing how much would have been lost to memory without those letters.

When I got married, my wife decided to carry on this tradition with our children. I was glad of this, but I almost felt like she had taken something from my side of the family for herself, which left me wondering what I could do that was unique for each of my children. I honestly don't know where this idea came from (other than perhaps my love of reading, particularly fiction), but I decided that I was going to write a novel for each of my boys, with them being the main character in their own story.

I had never even considered writing a novel before and did not consider myself the creative type. However, I have this tendency of following through on things that I set my mind to. In 2022, the first step in my plan came to fruition, and I published the novel I had written for my oldest son. The book that you're holding in your hand (or electronic device) is now my second book and is for my middle son. It's amazing how much work goes into this process, and I hope you enjoy the end result. I'm excited to give Justus an heirloom unlike what most kids ever receive from their parents. I sincerely hope he enjoys it.

I have a third son. So, one more book is forthcoming, which means I have another mountain to climb before it's done...

Acknowledgments

I have a number of people to thank for helping this book come to life. But I'll get to those good people in a moment. The first acknowledgment I'd like to make is to Books. I'd like to thank all the books I've ever read in my life. This may seem an odd thing to start off this section with, but I mean it in all sincerity. I was thinking recently on the things that have had the biggest impact on my life, and the top three are very clear in my life: my faith, my family, and reading.

I seriously cannot overstate the impact that reading has had on my life. My mom likes to tell the story of when I was four years old, I watched my older brother, Jason, learning how to read in Kindergarten. I was so excited to do what he was doing that I relentlessly pressed her to teach me how to read. She decided to call the grade school and see what they thought. Surprisingly, they counseled against it, as I would be too far ahead of my peers, might be bored in school and subsequently act up to keep myself occupied. As the story goes, I was inconsolable when my mom told me what the school said. Apparently, I decided that if the school wasn't going to teach me, I was going to teach myself. Although I don't remember this, my mom said that I actually began to teach myself to read, so she caved and taught me.

I never looked back. I have been a bibliophile ever since. Apparently, I loved books so much that, as a child, my cousins caught me reading a dictionary I found on the shelf at their house. I think I was about 6 years old at the time. It might be overstating the case that I've read anything I could get my hands on ever since, but it's probably not too far off. I remember grabbing books as a kid and pouring myself into the story. If it was non-fiction, I found it just as interesting. I loved learning about history and the world around me. Books gave me a sense of awe and wonder, and I'm grateful that they still do to this day.

When I finished my doctoral degree in psychology, I had essentially gone years without much recreational reading. Between a full-time doctoral program and working two part-time jobs to support us, I didn't have much time left. Once my degree was behind me, I suddenly had some free time on my hands. I decided that I was going to read as many books each year as my age was at the beginning of that year. So, if I was 30 years old on January 1st, my goal was to read at least 30 books that year. I've been doing this since 2006, and I've hit my goal every year. I'll have the privilege of aiming for more books every year, and that prospect is exciting to me.

I credit reading with the early development of my mind. I believe it nurtured my innate curiosity. It helped me develop a broad vocabulary. It filled my brain with so much information. I remember in high school, when someone would ask a factual question with our family present, my older brother Jason would often respond, "Ask Jared…he knows." Reading has given me a glimpse into the minds of some of the most amazing people. It's helped me think for myself and understand how important critical thinking is. It's given me a window to the universe and events (whether real or fantasy) that I could scarcely comprehend. I credit my insatiable thirst for knowledge to reading.

Reading is my favorite leisure time activity. I couldn't imagine my life without books. When I go to someone else's house, one of the first things I do is scan my surroundings for bookshelves. I'm a little saddened if I find none, but if I can find them, I spend my time looking through the books, while my wife, Rachel, is being social and probably wondering where I am. I'm often reading three or four books at once. For example, I'm currently reading the Bible, which I try to do on a daily basis. I'm reading Moby Dick. The book is nearly 700 pages, so I don't want to swamped down in one book for a while, so I'm reading a chapter a day until I complete it. Then I'm reading Stephen Lawhead's 'Byzantium', and that's the book that I'm plowing through during my free time. Often, the fourth book is something that I'm reading to my boys.

And I'm often trying to cram reading into small cracks in my schedule.

Rachel thinks I'm nuts, because I read when I brush my teeth. I read in between pitches when I'm watching baseball games on TV. I read between plays when I'm watching my son play baseball. Interestingly, when Justus (for whom this book is written) was playing middle school basketball, his teammates fell just short of placing bets with each other at the beginning of each game with how long it would take me to bust out my book and start reading.

Hopefully, I've stated my case effectively that reading has had an immense impact on me and has shaped my life in such a profound way that very few things ever have. I know that I would never have been able to complete a project like this without the influence and foundation that every book I've ever read has built in my life. So, thank you books for the role you've played in my life. I'm so much the better for it, and I'm looking forward to a very long and fruitful relationship with you going forward.

I'd also like to thank my parents, Al and Marie Detter, for laying the groundwork for my love of reading. They are ardent supporters of education and are both readers themselves. Without creating the fertile soil for my little mind, it wouldn't have grown like it did. I'd also like to sincerely thank them for taking the time to proofread the book and offer valuable suggestions to make it better.

No less worthy of acknowledgment, I'd like to thank my wife Rachel for all her support with this book. Writing and editing obviously is a time-consuming activity, and she is more than willing to give me that time. Thank you for tolerating my books and my inability to stop buying them. Thank you for not rolling your eyes anymore when you see me reading while brushing my teeth. Thank you for the time you took to proofread this book and offer your suggestions as well.

I'd also like to make mention of Kevin Baldizon, a long-time friend who shares my joy of reading. He has given me many great book recommendations, and I hope he feels the same way about me. Our frequent conversations over the years about books (and his critical thinking around them) has led me to trust him to proofread my two books so far. And, if you've ever written a book, you know how nerve-racking it can be to have a non-family member read your efforts. Kevin was instrumental in finding a plot hole in my book that I would not have been satisfied with, so thank you, Kevin, for taking the time and putting the effort in to make this a better story.

Not to be left out in all of the thankings, I'd like to thank Justus for coming into this world and making my world brighter for it. Thank you for being patient with me when I wouldn't tell you what the book title was until the last minute. I sincerely hope you enjoy this labor of love.

Finally, there are two groups I'd like to thank. First, I'd like to gratefully thank everyone who supported me on my Kickstarter campaign. In particular, I'd like to highlight the generosity of Al and Marie Detter, Jason and Beth Detter, Tracey Drake, Mike Barbee, and Mona Martin. Second, I'd like to thank the readers who thought this book worthy of reading. As I've said before, what is a book without a reader? I truly hope you enjoy it!

1

Moving In

The drive down the winding gravel road seemed longer than it had before. The excitement of purchasing a new home made them anxious to reach their destination, making the mile-long driveway seem to stretch on before them. In their excited state, they were almost too anxious to appreciate the beautiful woods that stood on the left side of the lane. The trees were tall and full of rich, green leaves. The birds, invisible in the foliage, sang loudly, announcing the late spring morning. Flowering dogwoods peppered the right side of the lane and created a boundary between the lane and a meadow accented with blooming wildflowers. It had rained the night before, and droplets blanketed the flora, creating a dazzling display of light when the sun peaked out from behind a cloud.

The sound of crunching gravel indicated that the vehicle was slowing down. They navigated the last curve prior to entering a circular driveway in front of the cottage that the newlyweds had just purchased. A small English garden was circumnavigated by the driveway and was highlighted by a fountain in its center, with four small paths bisecting the garden from the fountain to the driveway. The cottage itself was of stone and timber construction with a thatched roof. Ivy had a good head start up the sides of the building, reaching even higher where the chimney stood on the left hand side of the house. It was a two bedroom, one and a half story home with all of the quaint features of a cottage several centuries old, with the advantage of having been updated with modern conveniences. The young couple smiled as wisps of smoke escaped from the chimney, inviting them in to the comfort of their new home.

Justus pulled the car to a stop in front of his new home and helped his wife out of the car. Anna's delight was evident as she and her new husband approached the home that represented their new life together. Justus pulled open the front door, picked up his bride, and crossed the threshold, carefully placing Anna on the floor once inside the house. The happy couple embraced and shared their first kiss in their new home.

* * *

Justus was a 23-year old graduate student at Oxford with a focus on English medieval and renaissance literature. He had migrated from America several years before to study his favorite literature in its homeland and gain a greater appreciation for the geographical influences and origins of these writings. He was only in the country for several weeks when he had thoroughly fallen in love with the lakes, the hills, the valleys, the ancient country churches, the soaring Gothic cathedrals with their glorious stained glass, the small, country dirt roads, the villages of little cottages and row houses with their homey pubs, the massive stone castles, the crash of the grey Atlantic ocean on the sandy beaches, and the limitless stretches of cloud-swept skies, causing dappled sunlight to dance across the landscape.

As a child, he had always fantasized about going back in time and visiting England over Christmas, placing himself in Charles Dickens' *A Christmas Carol*. Despite several centuries' time since the days of Charles Dickens, there were places where Justus could walk down the street of a town with freshly fallen snow underfoot, a crisp December breeze in his face, his path lit by gas streetlamps down a road that was just what he had imagined as a child. He almost expected to see poor little Tiny Tim and the miserly Mr. Scrooge. He had decided he was never going back to live in America, his heart was so captivated by the juxtaposition of the old world and the modern day, the big city and the humble village. This decision was reinforced about six months into his graduate studies when he met Anna.

Anna was a junior at Oxford studying creative writing. She too was an American student studying abroad. She had distinguished herself with her studies in high school, so much so that she was offered a scholarship to this prestigious institution of higher learning. Jumping at the opportunity, she eagerly set off to begin her studies in England. Literature was highly valued in her household, which was filled with books. She was practically weaned on the great English writers and the imaginary worlds they produced; she entered the wardrobe with Lucy into C.S. Lewis' Narnia, she struggled alongside Frodo in Tolkien's Middle-earth, and she flew with Wendy in J.M. Barrie's Neverland. She would immerse herself in these new worlds and long to become part of the stories. As she matured, instead of becoming part of the stories, she found that she could pay homage to these authors and their worlds by creating stories of her own. There was no better place to develop her skills than on the island that nurtured her favorite authors. So, she spent her first two years in England dedicated to her studies.

It was during these years that Anna used the weekends to travel the countryside. She would visit the famous landmarks, tour the castles and manor houses, visit the gardens, and walk the small roads of the quaint villages. After seeing much of the country, she found that she developed strong preferences for a few of the places, and eventually one of the places tugged at her soul more than any other. She found a sense of tranquility in Glastonbury that she had never experienced before. She would head there on sunny, warm days and luxuriate in the sense that all was right in her world. She would lie down in the lush green grass and let the sun play over her skin as she drifted into a peaceful sleep. She would walk to the summit of Glastonbury Tor, gaze at the ruins of St. Michael's Tower, and daydream about the legendary Isle of Avalon, pretending, if just for a moment, that the legends were true, and she was standing on the Isle itself. She would take slow, meandering steps through the ruins of Glastonbury Abbey and allow herself to hope that Joseph of Arimathea really did found the first church in England just decades after the death of Christ and that he had brought the Holy Grail with him. She would find herself wishing that Arthur and

Guinevere really had been buried on these grounds. Weekdays would strain her patience, as she longed to return to this place, for it never ceased to renew her imagination and invigorate her spirit. And it was here where she first met Justus.

Justus had recently arrived in England several months before, and Anna had begun her third year of studies. She had predictably headed for Glastonbury early on the first sunny Saturday of the term. Deciding to spend the morning atop the Tor, she happily anticipated climbing the hill to its summit. Justus was touring the countryside, visiting all the sites associated with the legendary King Arthur and had decided to spend the day at Glastonbury.

Parking in Glastonbury, Justus walked up the rising streets that led to the base of the Tor. He carried a cheap paperback copy of Malory's Le Morte D'Arthur, feeling a thrill of finally seeing this legendary location in person. Just before departing the town and beginning his exploration of the Tor, he came across the Chalice Well, a spring that had brought forth its water, tinted red with iron oxide, for centuries. As he meandered around the well, he picked through his book, looking casually for references to Avalon. He turned to the end of the book and read about Arthur and Mordred's armies destroying themselves on each other until only Arthur and Mordred were left alive on the field of battle. Mordred was killed by Arthur but not before Arthur received a mortal wound to the head. Arthur was borne away across a lake to Avalon and was laid to rest at Glastonbury, although many did not believe in his death, choosing rather to believe that he would return at the time of England's greatest need. Justus concluded the chapter on Arthur's death by reading its final line, which was the inscription on Arthur's tomb, "HIC IACET ARTHURUS, REX QUONDAM REXQUE FUTURUS." Translating to English, he spoke softly aloud as he closed his book, "Here lies Arthur, the once and future king." As he spoke the last words, he noticed too late something moving right next to him, and he found himself bumping uncomfortably into it. His book tumbled from his hands and fell into one of the pools of the Chalice Well Gardens.

He looked up to notice a pretty face, made more striking by the look of surprise and embarrassment that often accompanies walking into someone, having not been watching were one was going. Figuring herself the guilty party and having seen his book tumble into the water, she began to apologize profusely.

"I'm so sorry," she exclaimed. "I wasn't even watching where I was going. I must have been daydreaming. I'm so sorry about your book." She bent down and picked the dripping book out of the water.

"I'm just lucky I brought a cheap reading copy, instead of the first edition." A bright smile of relief flashed across his face, as he was grateful the accident wasn't entirely his fault. The smile lingered, though, when he saw the attractiveness of this stranger. "I have to admit that I wasn't exactly watching where I was going either. My name's Justus, and I'll forget about my book if you tell me your name."

"My name is Anna," she said with a smile.

Justus felt butterflies in his stomach when she said her name. He could have sworn that the radiance of the sunshine infused her voice when she spoke. He gazed at her for a few seconds before he found his voice again, feeling embarrassed for helplessly staring in silence.

"Well Anna," his tongue finally loosening, "it's a pleasure to meet you. Seeing as the company I was planning to keep today ended up at the bottom of the pool, would you mind walking with me around the Tor?"

"It's the least I could do," her smile even brighter than before.

"I see by the lack of British accent that you're not from around here. Are you visiting?"

"No," she replied, suddenly concerned that Justus was just here on a vacation. "I'm a college student at Oxford. I'm in my third year there, studying creative writing. I'm actually here a lot, though. There's just something about Glastonbury that makes me happy."

"You go to Oxford?" Justus asked in a voice that betrayed more excitement than he had intended. "I'm just starting my graduate work there. I'm studying medieval and renaissance literature and was visiting some sites associated with the legend of King Arthur."

Anna tried to suppress a smile at the knowledge that she might be able to see Justus again and began to walk more quickly up the path to the Tor to hide her delight. Justus quickened his pace to catch up.

"Do you think this really was Arthur's Avalon?" Anna questioned happily.

"I know what the historians and archaeologists say, but maybe that's why I stay away from reading them. I think if we knew for sure one way or the other, it would diminish the mystery of it all, and the mystery fuels the imagination. Whether I truly believe it or not, I like the freedom to imagine that it was."

Anna smiled as his words. Justus had put concretely what she had felt only at an emotional level. She better understood now what drew her to this place, and she loved it all the more for it.

"I agree she said, and I love how you put it. Having the freedom to believe in something that may or may not be true is so much more romantic than having all the facts laid out before you. Not that I have an aversion to facts, but they don't feed the imagination as much." With those last words, she raced to the top of the Tor, with Justus again rushing to catch up, still clutching his wet book in her hand.

The breeze at the top caught her long brown hair, blowing it gracefully about her head. The slight coolness in the breeze and the exertion of rushing to the top brought a rosy color to her cheeks as she stood at the summit, catching her breath as Justus arrived shortly behind her. Her beauty was not lost on him, and the splendor of the surroundings only increased her attractiveness.

"You know, I'd love to see you again," he said, feeling that the risk of speaking boldly was worth communicating his interest in her.

"But we've only just arrived at the top, and I wasn't planning on leaving just yet," her demure smile lifting his hopes.

"I know, but for some reason I want to make sure that I'll see you again before I do anything else today."

"For now, let's spend the morning together, and if I still like you by lunch time, then I'll give you my number," she replied playfully.

The happy pair spent the rest of the morning and glorious afternoon in each other's company, engaging in small talk, laughing, sharing, and starting the journey of their relationship. Despite many happy days ahead, both looked back upon this day as the happiest, most magical day of their lives. Over the next year and a half, Justus courted Anna, slowly and irreversibly knitting their lives together.

It was toward the end of the spring semester of Anna's senior year that they were engaged. They took the first warm spring weekend and headed back to Glastonbury, itching to return to their favorite site for the first time in months, having been kept away by studies and a long winter. They luxuriated all day, walking through the town, meandering through the ruined abbey, picking wildflowers in the spring sunshine, and finally climbing the Tor in the early evening. They had just reached the top when Anna breathed deeply of the crisp air and said in a dreamy voice, "Look at the color of the sky, Justus. I love sunset on Glastonbury Tor." She turned back toward Justus to make sure he was appreciating the sky as well when she noticed that he was kneeling on the ground in front of her. It took her a moment to realize what was happening.

"Anna, this is where we first met and where I fell in love with you. There is no better place for me to express my desire to make my life with you and only you. I would be most honored if you would be my wife. Will you marry me?"

"Yes, I will marry you!" she exclaimed, her eyes sparkling with tears of joy.

As soon as Justus slipped the engagement ring on her finger, she pulled him up and they lovingly embraced, holding each other alone atop the Tor, framed against the background of St. Michael's Tower and the soft colors of the setting sun.

Now that they were engaged, there was plenty to do before they could get married. Anna had to graduate from Oxford and find a job. Anna was much too talented a writer and much too free a spirit to have a regular nine to five weekday job. She soon found work as a freelance writer and had some short stories published. She was good enough to earn a fair income this way and still have time to start her first novel, which she hoped to publish within several years. Justus had completed his first two years at the graduate school and had several more before completing his doctorate. He was excelling at his schoolwork, so much so that he was able to supplement Anna's income with regular tutoring appointments. All that was left was to find a home. They worked through that winter saving money to find a small place to live until they were more established. However, their parents surprised them with a sizable wedding gift, enough for a down payment on a nice home. Shortly thereafter they found their cottage.

"It's beautiful, isn't it?" Anna asked Justus as they saw it for the first time.

"It looks great, but I'd love to see it without all the snow."

"I can't believe our parents did this for us," Anna mused. "I guess I never really focused on the advantages of both of us being only children."

"It doesn't hurt that our parents aren't struggling for money either," he said with a smile.

The cottage was modest, but well maintained, and came with the services of a butler-gardener who seemed to be part of the place. Although the house had been vacant for a number of years, Clive had kept the house and grounds in pristine condition. He had served the previous owner so well and for so long that he had a small apartment built on the grounds and was given a stipend for life to maintain the property.

Justus and Anna fell in love with the house and decided to buy it. The closing was shortly before their late-spring wedding, and they spent the intervening weeks finishing their wedding plans and setting up the house to occupy after their nuptials. In fact, they were so excited to move in that they could think of no better honeymoon than just being together in their new home.

The day of their wedding came, and they professed their love in front of God, family, and friends. They spent the evening catching up with relatives from the States at the reception and retired for a good night's sleep to their hotel room, eager to start their life together in their new home on the next day.

They were so exhausted from their day that they slept right through the heavy spring rain that night and were finally awakened by shafts of sun, escaping from behind the clouds, coming through their hotel room window. They readied themselves and headed out in the crisp morning to go to their home for the first time as husband and wife.

* * *

"I see that Clive already has a fire on," Justus commented happily as he moved with his bride into their cottage.

"This is so wonderful," added Anna. "I never knew I could feel so happy. I love you, and I love our little cottage."

"I love you too," Justus replied. "I know we've been through the house before, but let's walk through it for the first time as husband and wife".

"I would love to," she said as they walked hand in hand through their lovely English cottage.

2

The Cottage

Clive was an older man of average build with gray and thinning hair, combed neatly to one side. He wore glasses perched across a sharp nose and had very active and alert eyes. His voice was steady and sure, and he was as dependable as they come. At 64 years of age, he was surprisingly lively and had a quick mind. He had worked at Ascalon Cottage since he was a youth and seemed so much a part of the landscape that things wouldn't be quite right without him. He knew everything there was to know about the cottage and the surrounding country. In fact, he had tended to the needs of the home and its owners for so long he seemed to be able to anticipate them, both for the house and the tenants.

This was the situation when Justus and Anna arrived at Ascalon Cottage for the first time as a married couple. A crackling fire was in the hearth, and a savory breakfast of eggs, bacon, sausages, and toast was nearly ready.

As they entered their home, they were reminded how thankful they were for the stewardship of the previous owners. Through the years, the modernization of the cottage disrupted the original state as little as possible. Justus and Anna relished the exposed wooden beams, the whitewashed walls, and the stonework.

The home was not large, but it contained a moderate size master bedroom, a small second bedroom, a relatively large eat-in kitchen, a sitting room, and a small drawing room up a narrow, wooden flight of stairs. Perhaps the most interesting room in the house, however, was the library. This room was actually off-limits when Justus and Anna had looked at the house. It was explained that it was a tradition going back to the original owners of the home that one had to actually own the home before having use of the library. They had seen pictures of the room before the purchase and were assured that the room was as pictured. In fact, it came written into the sales contract that they could void the purchase within thirty days of closing if the condition of the room dissatisfied them. They had been given the key at closing and had yet to use it.

"Good morning, Clive."

"Good morning, sir," he replied with his English accent. "Good morning to you too, madam."

"Good morning," Anna echoed happily.

Clive continued, "I've breakfast nearly finished. Please take your repose at the table, and I will serve you in a moment."

Justus and Anna took their seats at an old, wooden table, flanked on both sides by wooden benches, seemingly just as old as the table. They sat side-by-side facing the hearth, watching Clive dish out their steaming hot breakfast. The kitchen had a shallow, vaulted ceiling, with exposed wooden beams as trusses. The pots, pans, and dried herbs hanging from the beams were the perfect touch for a country cottage. The kitchen walls were mostly of stone, except on the wall adjoining the rest of the house. This one was whitewashed, standing in stark contrast to the grey stone of the other three walls. The floor was flagstone, which nicely complemented the large field stone hearth that Clive was using to cook breakfast.

"Here you are. I hope you enjoy my cooking, as you will likely be having plenty of it from now on," said Clive with a subdued smile, handing the steaming plates to Justus and Anna.

"Thank you. It looks and smells delicious, and I'm sure we will acquire a taste for your cooking," Anna replied with a playful grin.

After finishing breakfast and emptying the contents of their car into their bedroom, Justus was anxious to open the door to the library for the first time.

"Anna, let's go check out the library. I'm pretty curious to see what's inside," the anticipation thick in Justus' voice.

"You know, let's wait on the library. I think putting things off heightens the expectation sometimes, which makes the event more exciting when it happens. Plus I'd like to walk around the grounds first. It's a beautiful day, and I'm sure the sun is drying the grass. Let's go!" she said cheerily as she grasped Justus' arm and walked him toward the door.

Justus didn't have it in him to dampen the hopes of his new bride, especially with the look of such childlike excitement on her face. He suspected that she cared less about increasing their anticipation regarding the library and more about taking their first walk as husband and wife around their property and the surrounding countryside. Despite his impatience with having to wait to see the library, he was won over by the contagious enthusiasm of his wife and the beauty of their surroundings.

Anna took him by the hand and virtually skipped with happiness around to the back of the house. There was a small cottage garden abutting the house with its unkempt-by-design admixture of shrubs and flowers, all blazing with glorious spring blooms. They had a large lawn in the back, sprinkled with mature trees. A short field stone wall surrounded the property that appeared to be just as old as the house.

The couple lightly hopped the wall and landed in a lush, green meadow. Trees dotted the landscape, breaking the uniformity of the rolling, green hills. They walked along a path just outside of their stone wall that continued past the edge of their property. They soon came to a more heavily wooded area, dappled with sunlight, short grass, and moss. The sound of an unseen bubbling brook added to the pleasant ambiance of their walk. The path led them to a short footbridge that, spanning several dozen feet to the other bank, crossing the rivulet, which was making its way through a shallow gorge, deepening off to their right.

The bridge was sturdy and made of stone, practical in its construction, but quaint nonetheless. Justus and Anna paused on the bridge, admiring the stream and the lush green foliage covering its banks and the sides of the gorge.

"I didn't know we had water this close to the house," Justus mused.

"I didn't either; it can't be more than several hundred yards from the house. I think I'm going to like this spot. It's peaceful here, and I love the sound of running water. I feel like there's no one else in the world but us right now, and it makes me happy," Anna replied softly.

"Me too. What do you say we find out where this path takes us. We've got all day, or at least until we get hungry enough to turn back, whichever happens first."

Justus and Anna walked a mile or so along the path until it intersected with a country road, leading shortly to the small village nearest their home.

"Let's grab lunch at the pub. What do you say?" Justus queried, his stomach growling for nourishment.

"That's a great idea. You know, this all seems surreal to me. I never imagined that I would be living in England with my new husband, walking through the beautiful countryside to eat lunch at a quaint pub. It seems too perfect."

"I know what you mean," he replied. "I hope I never get to the point where I take any of this for granted."

They happily lunched on the local fare and made the return journey home, taking a long leisurely stroll through the countryside down small country roads. Afternoon had turned to evening before the spell the land had cast on them was broken by growling stomachs. They made short work of the rest of their journey, ready to eat dinner.

"Clive, I hope you didn't prepare us lunch or expect us for an early dinner," Anna said with a touch of concern in her voice. "I didn't even think to mention how long we might be gone, and we ate lunch at the pub."

"Not to worry, madam. I presumed that you and the mister would be gone for a good spell. I did not prepare a lunch. I can have a passable dinner ready for you within the half hour if you would like to freshen up. I already have something on for you."

Justus and Anna washed up and sat down to a wonderful meal of roast lamb, potatoes, and baby carrots. Thick slices of bread and warm butter were washed down by cold, refreshing water. After dinner, they sat in peaceful silence, their hunger sated, enjoying the warmth of their kitchen.

"Well," began Justus. "I don't know about you, but I'm pretty worn out from our long walk today. I'd like to check out the library and then hit the sack. What do you say?"

"That's a great idea. I'm pretty tired too, but I've kept you too long from the room. I'm excited to see what's in there myself."

The library was in the back right-hand corner of the cottage, with an ancient looking wooden door in the center of the curved wall separating the library from the rest of the house. A large metal key was given to them at the closing to unlock the door. Justus was anticipating a little effort to turn the lock, but he was surprised to see that it turned smoothly, like it was brand new. He grasped the iron ring that served as a door handle and pushed the door open. The ambient light allowed Justus to see the light switch just inside the room. When he turned the light on, he was amazed at what he saw.

The room was brightly lit by a large chandelier, consisting of a plain, black iron ring with dozens of electric candles spread evenly around it. The room itself was octagonal and, with the exception of the doorway, was completely lined with bookshelves, filled to capacity with antique books. The bookshelves were of a strikingly rich mahogany and stretched from the floor to the base of the low-pitched conical ceiling from which the chandelier hung. The floor to the center of the ceiling was fourteen feet, and the bookshelves were a full ten feet tall. Given the height of the bookshelves, each section of the octagon was equipped with its own rolling ladder, angled out far enough to give clearance to a protruding shelf and cabinets that comprised the bottom three feet of the bookshelves. The cabinet doors were all bedecked with lead-paned beveled glass.

Beautiful, dark hardwood floors complemented the mahogany bookshelves and matched the wood in the ceiling. A thick, circular oriental rug was placed in the center of the room and was at least 12 feet in diameter, covering the inner two-thirds of the wooden floor. Upon the rug was an ornately carved chaise lounge, two large and very comfortable looking armchairs, and a high-back couch, all looking inward on an equally ornate large, low center table.

The room was exquisite, and Justus and Anna just stood for a moment in the doorway slack-jawed before Anna broke the silence.

"I can't handle this tonight. My brain and my body are telling me two different things. I'm worn out from the walk, but I'd never go to bed if I took one more step into this room. I think I need to get some sleep, and I'll tackle this room tomorrow when I'm fresh and rested."

"Are you sure, honey? I'm going to stay up and look around. I couldn't go to sleep now if my life depended on it."

"I know. I'd love to stay up with you, but I'm too tired to appreciate the room tonight, and I'd be too excited to want to leave if I got started. I've got all day tomorrow to spend in here." They kissed goodnight, and she departed for bed, leaving Justus alone to explore the library.

After Anna left, Justus stood in shock for several more minutes. This library was probably worth more than the rest of the house, and he was having a difficult time wrapping his mind around the fact that he actually now owned it. He then proceeded to the center of the room and slowly rotated himself in a complete circle to see the library 'in the round'. While he was doing this, he realized that the open door broke the continuity of the room, so he shut the door and re-focused his attention on the amazing library. He went to a bookshelf and touched the smooth wood. The dark, rich tone of the wood reminded him of what he might find in a country house of a nobleman. He browsed a section of books, finding them all to be in near perfect condition, many of them appearing to be rather valuable antiques. The majority of the books were from the 18th and 19th centuries, but some went back to the late medieval era, such as a complete illuminated book of hours from Paris, finished in 1452. A fair number of folios were from the 16th and 17th centuries, more often than not written in Latin.

After sampling many of the books in the library, Justus couldn't resist what he had always wanted to do since he was a little boy - climb the rolling library ladders. He climbed each ladder in the room and pulled a few books out, finding a volume in English from 1763 on botany in the British Isles. Another volume was a 19th century historical account of Queen Boadicea and her Celtic revolt against the Romans.

He climbed the ladder on the final bookshelf and pulled a volume from the shelf that had caught his eye. The book appeared to be extremely old, although in virtually perfect condition. It had soft calfskin pulled over boards with five horizontal ridges down the spine. The front board was stamped in the center just above the midline with a rampant dragon enclosed in a circle of intertwining lines - an endless knot of Celtic design. He opened the book, and the pages were white and supple, like it had just been printed. Each leaf was immaculately illuminated, the turn of virtually every page revealing a new work of art.

Justus carefully cradled the book and slowly descended the ladder, sitting in a plush armchair to more closely examine it. He gently traced his fingers over the leather binding, following the contours of the stamp on the cover. Carefully, he opened the cover and looked again at the first page. Justus almost jumped when he took a closer look. What had originally been written in a language he did not recognize had transformed into English. The words seemed to morph themselves before his eyes, but the change seemed to be so subtle that he began to doubt that he had actually seen anything at all.

Enraptured by this amazing book, Justus settled himself comfortably in his chair and began to read.

3

Strange Beginnings

"Hold fast, miscreant knave! Dress arms and fight!"

Justus was aware of little, except for something heavy encasing his head, a blinding strip of light directly in his eyes, an unsure seat, and yelling coming from somewhere in front of him.

"You have been fair warned, vagrant. Ha!!"

Justus heard the sound of approaching hooves and was able to lift a visor from in front of his face, only to see what looked like a knight on horseback charging him with a lance leveled at his chest. He had barely enough time to raise a shield he found on his left arm before the lance struck. With a ferocious jolt, Justus was sent head over heals off the back end of the horse upon which he had been sitting and hit the ground with a crash. Feeling like he had just been struck by a car, Justus scarcely lifted his head off the turf when the knight leapt from his horse, unsheathed his sword and stood over him.

"Ne'er have I seen such a cowardly knave. Doff your helm so I can lop off your head."

Justus was stunned into silence, unable to utter any words in his defense, feeling like his throat had closed up.

"Come man. I have not all day. Choose death or yield and swear me fealty, but make haste."

The offer of fealty snapped Justus back into action, "I yield! I yield!"

"Well, stand up and let me discover what manner of knight is before me. By the Rood! I ha' ne'er beheld such an ill-prepared knight. I know not what advantage your fealty bears me, but take it I will." With that, Justus felt himself bodily lifted from the ground and stood on his feet.

"Mount your horse and follow where I lead."

Justus clumsily climbed on his horse while the knight swiftly mounted his and waited for Justus to ride up to him. After waiting several moments, the knight exclaimed, "Truly you are testing my patience. What causes you to dally now?"

"I'm sorry, but my horse won't go," was all Justus could reply.

"I should have lopped off your head when I had the chance," the knight proclaimed while he rode to Justus' horse. He quickly tied the bridle to his saddle and led Justus and his horse across the meadow, through a wooded glade, and into a large field, crowned with a hilltop stronghold.

A winding path led across a small stream at the bottom of the hill and up to wooden gates, connected to timber palisades that surrounded the dwelling. Sentries at the gates allowed the knight and Justus to pass through to the interior of the compound.

Inside of the palisades was a large wooden hall, several outbuildings and lesser dwellings, a number of peasants, men-at-arms, and grazing livestock. The knight dismounted and ordered Justus down as well.

Calling to a man close at hand, he said, "Take these horses and water them well, and come you with me," pointing at Justus as he finished the sentence.

Justus' head was reeling with the events of the last half hour. It was just sinking in that he barely escaped with his life and now he had no idea what plans this knight had for him. Trying to not show his fear, Justus followed the knight into the hall. A servant helped the knight remove his armor as he began talking.

"My name is Lord Alden. I have earned my lands and title through valiant service to mine king. My deeds are sung in many halls, and I am not a man who brooks insolence. Tell me the name of my new servant."

"My name is Justus, Lord Alden. I'm not a knight, and I don't really know how I ended up on that horse."

"You are truthful in saying you are no knight. After I sup, we shall venture outside to see if a knight you will be or if a servant's cloths are more befitting you."

Lord Alden dined on roast pig and cheese served on a trencher with a wooden cup filled with ale. He eyed Justus curiously during the course of the meal, as if he was unsure whether or not he should have accepted his fealty. He then decided that all would be revealed in the tests he would require Justus to perform after the meal, and he finished off his food with a will.

"Now get you outside, and we shall see what it is you are made of," Lord Alden proclaimed as he rose from the bench. "Your fate is upon you and will determine in what capacity you shall serve me.

"Five tests will you perform: riding, sword fighting, archery, the quarterstaff, and grappling. Now let us out into the clean air and see what we will."

With much trepidation, Justus followed Lord Alden into the sunshine, not knowing what the day was going to hold for him. They walked to the stables where a horse was waiting, and Lord Alden bade him mount.

"You must needs ride this steed to that yonder oak tree and return to this place with as much speed as you can muster. Now get you hence!" and he smacked the rump of the horse, causing it to leap into a run, jostling Justus briefly before he went tumbling off.

Lord Alden laughed heartily as he picked Justus up and corralled his horse. "Well, riding is no strength of yours, as these two falls have borne witness. Let us see how you do handle a sword."

He led Justus to a small fenced-in area where a squire was waiting with two broad swords, handing one to Justus and keeping one for himself.

"Fear not, Justus, the edges are blunted and my squire has been instructed to strike with the flat of the sword. This is no fight to the death. Commence!"

The squire slowly approached and Justus retreated tentatively until he was stuck in the corner of the enclosure. The squire then presented Justus with a series of swings and thrusts, showing little refinement in his swordplay, but it was enough to send the sword flying from Justus' hands, leaving him defenseless.

"Enough!" roared Lord Alden. "Methinks I know where you shall end up in my house, but we must finish the test. Pick you up the bow and arrows against yonder fence. Let us see if your fortunes change when flinging bolts."

Justus picked up the bow and arrows and followed his new master to the edge of a field, where a rough target was painted on a bale of hay. Justus looked questioningly toward Lord Alden and received a slight nod of the head in answer. Justus notched an arrow to the bow and shot. The first arrow was sped at such a low angle, that it went into the ground well short of the target. Justus notched the second arrow and angled the bow upward to compensate for the low angle of the last shot. This time, the arrow arced high into the air, still landing well short of the target.

"I have seen enough," grumbled Lord Alden. "Your lack of skill in these arts I find no longer amusing. Get you hence to the enclosure, and we will test your skill with the quarterstaff."

With wounded pride and fear over what his failures might mean for his immediate future, Justus followed him back into the enclosure, where the same squire stood with two quarterstaffs and a smug look of confidence on his face.

"Proceed!" Lord Alden called, as the squire tossed the quarterstaff to Justus.

Having felt Justus out with the swordplay, the squire was feeling confident in his abilities to overmatch the newcomer. He was also looking for an easy way to impress his master with a victory. He rushed at Justus to make a quick end to the fight, swinging his quarterstaff wildly. Justus ducked quickly and swung his staff into the exposed ribs of the squire, doubling him over in pain. Justus made a short, quick swing and snapped the squire sharply in the hamstrings, bringing him to his knees.

Lord Alden chuckled at the unexpected result, "Pride cometh before a fall, 'tis said. Next time, get a better measure of your opponent, young squire." Turning to Justus he said, "At least one of the tests you have passed, but 'tis against my youngest squire. Let us see how you do fare against your new master."

Lord Alden dismissed the defeated squire out of the square enclosure, and he pulled off his tunic, exposing his torso. He was well muscled and imposing, despite the small paunch at his belly. None of the other tests made Justus as anxious as this one, as he was now facing a large, experienced fighter, not knowing what would happen to him if he lost. In some ways, Justus felt like he was fighting for his life.

Lord Alden addressed Justus, squatting slightly at the knees, feet staggered and about shoulder length apart, "Let us see if you are man enough to tangle with a true warrior." With that, he made a charge at Justus.

Justus was similarly crouched, but he was not brimming with bravado, as Lord Alden was. His eyes were wide, drawing in every detail. His ears became sensitive to every sound, and it seemed as if time slowed down. Although Lord Alden was approaching rapidly, it was as if he was moving toward Justus in slow motion. Justus' senses were so heightened in the moment that he seemed to be able to anticipate the moves of his opponent.

Justus nimbly ducked and spun away from his attacker, causing his opponent to completely miss his target. Lord Alden turned quickly and approached again. This time, he was more cautious with the attack and as Justus ducked again, Lord Alden grabbed his ducking shoulder and shoved. Knocked off balance, Justus fell to one knee and dove forward into a roll, avoiding his pursuer. Despite Justus' heightened awareness, Lord Alden was relentless, especially now that he had misjudged his new servant. Onlookers had gathered around to watch, and he was determined to uphold his pride. In this he was aided by Justus' caution. While Lord Alden was the attacker, Justus was too fearful in the moment to engage in much more than defensive maneuvers.

Finally, filled with frustration, Lord Alden charged Justus again. He swung his right arm back to land a crushing blow, when Justus spun to his right. Having studied Justus' strategy thus far, this was what Lord Alden was counting on. He landed a stinging left hand in the middle of Justus' back, knocking him face down in the dirt. Justus rose quickly, but not quickly enough to avoid the bulk of his new master from leaping on top of him. Desperate, Justus attempted to buffet the flanks of Lord Alden with quick punches, while Lord Alden worked to control Justus' arms. He finally grabbed him around both wrists, attempting to stop the punching, but Justus fought all the more furiously. Justus kicked his legs, throwing up his hips and almost succeeded in sending Lord Alden head first on to the ground. He did succeed in unbalancing his attacker enough that he let go of Justus' right hand, which came thundering down heal first on Lord Alden's chest, knocking him further off balance. Justus freed up his other hand and heaved his opponent off sideways.

Without waiting an instant, Justus grabbed him from behind, locked his hands around Lord Alden's torso and began to squeeze. Lord Alden was not used to finding himself at a disadvantage and began to struggle furiously. He kicked backward but to no effect. He tried to break Justus' hold with no results. Finally, starting to feel concerned that he was weakening from lack of air, he threw his head back violently, hitting Justus square in the nose. Blood burst forth, and he was blinded by the pain and tears that filled his eyes. He involuntarily released his hold and was thrown to the ground. Justus covered his nose with both of his hands and was writhing in pain.

"Do you yield?" demanded Lord Alden. Hearing no response, "Do you yield!! If not, then we shall continue."

"I yield," choked Justus through the blood and tears that were cutting rivulets in the dust on his face.

"You have been kicked from two horses and have yielded twice in the same day - unfortunate, indeed! I may yet be able to salvage you, though. You are passing strong and a good fighter. Some training at the other arts and you might survive your first battle," he said with a laugh and smacked him on the shoulder.

A maid servant was fetched to clean Justus up and make him presentable again. Justus followed her to the stream, took the cloth he was given, and wiped the blood from his face. After several minutes more of pinching his nose and wiping with the cloth, the blood flow finally ebbed. He rinsed the cloth off in the stream, wiped the dust off the rest of his face, and cleaned his hands as much as possible. Leading him to a small outbuilding, the maidservant gave Justus rough brown wool pants, soft leather shoes, a stained but clean white shirt, and a brown leather jerkin. He was then led back into the lord's hall.

Several men had just arrived on horseback and were standing before Lord Alden as he sat on a carven chair on a dais at the end of his hall. There were two large men, both with long hair, one blonde, one brown, both with full beards, and dressed in battle gear. Two less imposing men stood behind them, and Justus was to find out later that they were squires.

"Ah, Justus, come forward and learn your fate," called out Lord Alden with a twinkle in his eye.

Justus glanced quickly at the maidservant whose expressionless face gave him no comfort. He moved forward cautiously and approached the men, who were all now looking at him.

"Bana, Logan, look you upon mine new warrior," Lord Alden stated, flicking his wrist toward Justus. "Logan, Justus is to be your shadow. You are a worthy warrior and from you he will learn the art of war. Train him tirelessly and train him well."

With that, the man with the blonde hair stepped forward. He flashed a quick smile toward Justus, and Justus warmed to him instantly. Logan had a strong, but open and honest, face. Behind the proud eyes, he had the kind look of someone who was not too far removed from his days of training to forget what they were like.

"Bana, you will remain with me and relay what news you have."

With that, Logan led Justus from the hall, understanding that his lord's address to Bana meant that he was no longer needed. Justus was secretly pleased that Bana was remaining behind. Bana's face looked hard and proud; not the kind pride that Justus recognized in Logan. Bana's pride looked dangerous.

"What say you, young warrior?" Logan said with a bright smile. "Methinks Lord Alden means to use you for good purpose. Not many escape his grasp with but blood on the nose."

"I have no idea what he wants me for, but I'm afraid I'll find out all too soon."

"What a strange manner of speech you have. Your home must needs be beyond these borders."

"You have no idea," replied Justus; the unintentional irony was not lost on him.

"You did hear Lord Alden. Your training is to begin immediately. Get you some drink for refreshment, and we shall begin."

4

Illness

The sunlight was pouring through Justus and Anna's bedroom window, waking Anna up early the next morning. She groaned mildly at the headache that greeted her, and she rolled over to see if Justus was awake. To her surprise, he was not there. She had slept the night away by herself. She quickly sat up, only serving to make her headache throb. With her hand against her head, she swung her legs out of bed to search for her errant husband. She quickly decided to look for him in the last place she left him - the library.

"Justus, wake up. You've been sleeping in the library all night," she said as she shook her husband awake.

"What? In the library? What do you mean?" was all he could muster as he attempted to clear the mental cobwebs. Sitting up, he took in his surroundings and remembered his exploration of the library the night before.

"Oh!" he said with some surprise. "I didn't mean to fall asleep in here. You mean I've been in here all night? What time is it?"

"It's after eight o'clock. I thought you were coming to bed last night."

"So did I. I didn't mean to fall asleep in here. I remember exploring the bookshelves and pulling a book that looked interesting. I sat down to read it, and I don't remember much after that. I must have been more tired than I thought. Although, I do remember having a really strange dream last night.

So vivid…"

"If you don't mind, let's talk about your dream later. I woke up with a real splitter. Do you know where we packed the Tylenol?" They left the library in search of headache relief and breakfast, the latter of which Clive was working on in the kitchen.

"Good morning," Clive said, greeting them happily as they entered the kitchen. "I trust you both slept well."

"Yeah, that's weird," responded Justus. "I slept pretty well, but I guess I was in the library all night. And I had the weirdest dream…"

"And I woke up with a headache," Anna interposed. Hopefully a good breakfast and some Extra Strength Tylenol will fix that for me."

They ate their breakfast in silence, as Clive seemed to be observing them from across the kitchen.

"Clive, why don't you join us for breakfast," offered Justus.

"No thank you, sir. I ate before you awoke. My appetite is sated for the time being. How did you find the library last night, sir?"

"Oh, it's beautiful. I've never seen anything like it in my life. And the books must be worth a fortune. So many books, and so old too. I found this interesting book last night that I started to read… You know, I don't remember much about what I read. Or maybe I don't remember much about the dream. I can't really remember which was which. Such a strange dream, and it seemed so real too."

"Well, I'd like to see the library after breakfast," said Anna, her rekindled interest seeming to dull some of the pain of her headache. "I was too worn out last night, Clive. I went to bed, leaving Justus to explore. As a matter of fact, I'll go have a look right now," she said as she pushed her empty plate from her. "Will you come with me, love?"

"Absolutely!" replied Justus as he shoved the last bite of breakfast in his mouth. "You'll know where to find us, Clive, if you need us."

Justus followed Anna into the library and was just as excited this morning as he was the previous night.

"It truly is beautiful," the awe obvious in Anna's voice.

"You don't know the half of it," Justus replied. "Some of these books go back to the late medieval era, although most of them are more recent than that. But virtually none of them are newer than the 1800s – and many are older. All the books are in such good condition, too."

Anna smiled at Justus. She loved to see him "gushing" over the library. They both shared a love for books, and she was so happy to see her beloved husband pleased.

"Let me show you the book I was reading last night." Justus walked to the big armchair in which he slept last night to get the book. Not seeing the book, he looked for it on the other furniture in the room.

"That's odd," Justus mused aloud. "Did I have a book this morning when you woke me up?"

"No, I didn't see any book. Are you sure you didn't put it away?"

"I fell asleep in that chair reading it, so unless I put it away in my sleep, it should be there."

"Where did you get the book?" asked Anna trying to be helpful.

"On the top shelf over here by the door." He climbed the ladder to the top shelf to show where he pulled the book when he paused. "That's weird. The book's up here. I wonder how it got back."

"You must have just forgotten that you put it back. That's all."

"I could have sworn I didn't put the book away before I fell asleep. That's so strange…"

Justus and Anna spent much of the rest of the day exploring the library and showing each other the treasures they discovered. Despite the adventure in book finding they were sharing, the excitement was only serving to worsen Anna's headache.

"All this excitement, not to mention the headache, has left me drained. I'm going to turn in after dinner. I'm sure I'll feel fine in the morning," Anna said as they sat down for supper.

"I really hope you do feel better, honey. We haven't even gotten through half the books yet."

Anna was true to her word and headed off to bed after supper. Justus decided to spend more time in his prized library, and Clive had some errands to run for the remainder of the evening. Justus ascended the ladder, grabbed the mysterious book from last night, again admiring the beautiful illuminations, settled back down into the chair, and began to read.

* * *

"Your bones had best be strong, for they soon will be rattled," a broad smile crossed Logan's face as he slapped Justus on the back. "My lord has given me a twelvemonth to properly train you. You are exceeding late in life to commence martial training, but we shall see what time and some sweat can produce. Horsemanship shall be our first pursuit."

Logan led Justus to the stables to choose a horse for him. He demonstrated how to saddle and bridle a horse, and they walked to a flat, open field immediately adjacent to the compound.

"Word has traveled about the trouble you had handling your steed. No charger have I chosen for you yet. Rather a palfrey should suit first."

Justus made a rather ungainly attempt at mounting the horse, much to the amusement of his teacher. The second attempt was no more graceful, but Justus found his seat.

"If you can not get your horse to move, then your horse is no worldly good to you. Thus, the first lesson."

Logan spent the whole day teaching Justus to coax the horse into a walk and then a canter. Once cantering, Logan rode alongside Justus on his own horse to ensure that Justus never lost control of the reins. As evening drew to a close, Justus dismounted the palfrey and stretched out his aching legs.

"I don't know how you can ride for so long. I don't think I'll be able to walk tomorrow."

"Then we shall pursue an exercise that will ease the burden on your legs. We shall see what skill with the arrows."

After dinner, Justus went to bed early, sleeping on the floor in the great hall with the other men who served Lord Alden. Despite only straw between him and the hard dirt floor of the hall, Justus was so exhausted that he slept undisturbed until morning.

* * *

"Wake up, you sluggard!" roared Logan goodheartedly as the morning sun was rising. "Get you up, we must needs make a warrior out of you -and no small task that is."

Justus nearly cried out in pain as he attempted to stand, and he could only hobble after Logan as they went to the armory to begin the day's archery lesson. Logan laughed good naturedly at Justus' obvious discomfort all the way out to the archery range.

Justus had little more success this day than he did under Lord Alden's test. Justus drew many a laugh from his teacher, but he bore it patiently, knowing that there was no malice in it. As with the previous day, all day was spent in exercise and Justus went to bed early again.

Just before he turned in, Logan said, "You are fortunate the Sabbath is on the morrow. Your soft muscles could use a day to recover." He walked away chuckling to himself, and Justus fell asleep with a smile of relief on his face.

Justus could do little but lie around and nurse his sore muscles the next day. The soreness in his legs had not abated, and his arms, shoulders, and back were virtually useless. He did not rise from his bed until the families on the compound were returning from mass.

"You are a sluggard, Justus," laughed Logan as he returned to the hall. "A little riding, a little archery and you do remain abed all day." Despite his words, Justus was required to do no work all day, as Logan wanted him as fresh as possible to begin training again in the morning.

The next six months happened thus, with daily martial training, with the exception of the Sabbath and other holidays. Over time, Justus proved to be an apt pupil, his muscles hardening and his confidence improving. Justus was politely ignored by all at the settlement, with the exception of his constant companion and teacher, Logan, who explained to Justus that Lord Alden had declared that he must be left alone during his training until such time that he was proven worthy to join the settlement as a full member. Such an opportunity presented itself during the beginning of the seventh month of Justus' training.

Justus was awakened by Logan in the misty darkness that presaged the coming dawn. Justus wiped the sleep from his eyes and stood groggily in the hall of his liege lord.

"We shall see what manner of warrior I have made you in these six months," Logan spoke in a low but excited tone.

"What are you talking about? And why are you waking me up so early? We don't usually start until the sun is up."

"We hunt today! You have been kept apart from the rest for the purpose of your training, but today I deem you ready to join in the noble exercise of the hunt. You have made progress in all your training and are wonderly good with your horse. Forsooth, you are nigh upon my skill as a rider. You have also progressed apace with the bow, sword, and spear. Thus, I have deemed you ready and presented my petition before Lord Alden on yesterday's eve. He agreed! Ha!" his voice rose with the last words and he slapped Justus across the back. He quickly lowered his voice with a sheepish grin, so as not to wake the women and children. "Lord Alden has been watching you, and methinks he approves of your pitiful hide." His smile belied his affection for his pupil. "Now get you awake and let us hence."

Logan led Justus to the armory and handed him a jerkin of hardened leather to put over his shirt, along with hardened leather greaves and gauntlets. Once dressed, Logan handed Justus a quiver full of arrows, a bow, a throwing spear, and a short sword. Once fully equipped, Logan brought Justus a palfrey from the stables, whereupon Justus affixed the spear to the saddle, slid the sword in his scabbard, and fastened the quiver and bow to his back. After mounting, Justus watched Logan ready himself through the grey mist that still clung to the landscape.

All around him, Justus could hear other men preparing themselves and see their shadowy movements in the darkness. Logan and Justus rode to the meeting point, where ten other men were to ride out hunting. The hunting dogs whined with anticipation, eager to be loosed into the woods.

Justus' heart quickened from his nervousness when Lord Alden called out, "Good men, 'tis a fair morn for hunting." This brought some chuckles from the men, and Justus shivered involuntarily from the cool air and the mist condensing on his skin. "A herd of roe deer crosses these lands of late, and my palate craves venison. A new spear to the one who takes the greatest stag." Loud cheers arose from the men, who were getting anxious to hunt. "We will ride quietly north. The herd was last seen four leagues from here, but we dare not lose the element of surprise. May God speed our mounts in the chase and make our arrows and spears aim true." With that, Lord Alden turned and slowly led his men down the hill, out of his enclosure, and north into a nearby wood.

Logan waited until all of the men had ridden after Lord Alden and brought up the rear with Justus. They rode side by side in silence about twenty yards behind the other men and had done so for about fifteen minutes before Logan spoke.

"Justus, you are a mystery. You were attired as a knight but showed no skill when challenged by our liege lord. Your manner of speech is strange, and even you know not from whence you came. This day is more than a simple hunt for you. This day is the end of the mystery. What you were no longer matters; it is what you will become that is before you.

"When Lord Alden commissioned me to train you, he had already made firm in his mind that no servant would you be. He saw something goodly in you and set you apart for martial training. Your training does not end today, but no longer are you set apart. Today is your initiation into Lord Alden's rule. You will continue to train with me until the twelvemonth is complete, but you are now under his command and must do his will.

"If you do complete this hunt with honor, then you will be a warrior serving Lord Alden. As such, I must impart to you knowledge that will serve you well in your new role. First and foremost, you must know your place. Being a warrior is a place of honor and must be upheld with honor. The women, children, and servants must needs treat you with honor, and this honor must be returned. A warrior who serves his lord necessarily serves his people. Forget this not. Although a warrior is not without honor, he does not possess the highest honor. We serve at Lord Alden's pleasure, and we must call him by his title, as Lord Alden must with his liege. The order of knighthood is also an honor above that of the warrior. Knights serve at the pleasure of their lord, but they are also his counselors and leaders in battle.

"Justus, I am one of Lord Alden's knights, and he has placed you in my care. As such, after this hunt, you must publicly honor my position and must not forget yours. I will continue your training, but it will be as knight to warrior. Knights are referred to as 'sir' by those under them, their fellow knights, and their lieges. Do you understand?"

Justus silently nodded his head as they plodded on through the wood. He did not feel it was his place to yet speak, so he kept his silence.

"As a warrior in training, you will continue your martial exercises daily with me. However, should our lord need your services, then you will perform such services as he requires.

"Should you conquer another warrior or knight, either in battle or in single combat and your foe lives, then you must honor your foe, even in his defeat. He must needs be given the choice to yield or to die. If your opponent chooses to die, then you are duty bound to honor his choice. The spoils of the battle belong to Lord Alden, and he will honor your efforts as he sees fit. If it be a knight you defeat, and he does not yield, then upon his death, all those under his command are disbanded, free from his service. You can surely see the blow this is to the knight's liege.

"However, if your opponent chooses to yield, it is to your lord they must swear fealty. If it be a knight who does yield to you, then that knight and all those under him must swear fealty to your lord. They are then honor bound to serve their new liege lord to their utmost. In order to reclaim his lost men, the former lord must conquer the new one. Only then will his previous retainers be free to give him back their loyalty.

"As a warrior, your rewards come solely from the generosity of your lord. Not so as a knight. A knight is highly honored and more rewarded in battle. Should a knight conquer a warrior in battle who yields, the warrior then swears fealty to the knight. Should a knight conquer a fellow knight in battle who yields, the knight then swears fealty to the knight, as do all those who call him liege. Thus, a conquering knight may very quickly amass a small army, all who serves the knight, who in turn serves his lord. Half of a knight's plunder is his lord's and half he keeps as his own. Many aspire to be a knight;

few succeed. Valor and honor are the hallmarks of knighthood, but success is what makes a knight. An unsuccessful knight is a dead knight. Thus, you must continue to train."

The party arrived at a small vale in the woods and paused for refreshment before gathering around Lord Alden. "We shall ride in pairs, sweeping through the wood parallel to one another, stirring the deer. Sound your horn when quarry has been sighted, and Godspeed." With that, the men rode off two by two through the woods in pursuit of the hunt.

5

A New Discovery

Clive's voice awoke Justus from his sleep in the library, "Good morning sir, your wife has sent me to summon you to her. She is again not feeling well. Should I prepare you breakfast?"

"Yeah sure, that'd be great... I can't believe I fell asleep in the library again. And my dream. So odd. They have been so real the last two nights."

Justus made his way into his bedroom to find Anna propped up on the bed, with a wan look to her face. "Are you feeling okay, honey? You're looking a little sick today."

"I really don't feel well," Anna replied. "My headache feels worse, and I have some nausea. I'm hoping a little rest today will have me feeling better."

"Have you had breakfast yet?"

"No, I don't really feel very hungry right now."

"You should eat *something*," Justus replied. "You need to get some calories in you to keep your strength up."

"I know. It's just that the way I'm feeling right now, I'm not very motivated to eat anything."

"I'll have Clive bring you something light, and we can have breakfast in bed this morning."

Anna smiled softly at her husband's concern, as he walked from the room to get breakfast. Justus soon returned to the bedroom with food and spent most of the morning by his wife's side, talking about their new lives together, helping Anna to focus on something other than how she was feeling.

After lunch, Anna relieved Justus of his bedside duty, encouraging him to enjoy the day, as she wished to take a nap. Justus walked outside to enjoy the beautiful spring weather and found himself replicating the walk that he and Anna took their first day in the house. Once he reached the bridge over the small gorge, he decided to do some exploring. To his left, he found a place that was less steep than the surrounding sides, which allowed him to descend.

He alighted on a large, flat stone protruding out into the brook, which caused a pleasant disruption in the flow of the water. The sound of the water was louder than on the bridge, but it was not so loud as to drown out the songs of the birds roosting in the trees growing from the walls of the gorge and in the woods above. Rocks, small trees, flowers, and shrubs dotted the sides of the ravine and occasionally were found along the bottom in deposits of soil outside the brook's course. Having climbed down twenty or so feet below the level of the woods, Justus suddenly felt completely isolated from the rest of the world. It was as if his line of sight was all that existed, time virtually standing still for him and the brook bubbling through the gorge.

Justus followed the brook under the bridge, enjoying his little slice of tranquility, drinking in every step he took along the bank. He walked for about fifty feet without any noticeable difference in the terrain, when the ravine started pulling to the right and at a steeper decline. In addition to the sound of more swiftly running water, he could discern the sound of water falling. Around a bend, Justus discovered the source of the sound. There was a small waterfall, cascading down to meet the brook again about fifteen feet below. Justus carefully picked his way down some large rocks adjacent to the waterfall, in order to continue his course alongside the brook.

By this time, the gorge walls had grown to nearly fifty feet above the bottom, with the steep walls only serving to increase Justus' sense of solitude. He meandered slowly by the water, with the soft turf underfoot and the slice of blue sky overhead until he encountered another bend. Shortly after making this turn, he came across what looked like a small cave on the right hand side of the ravine. He scrambled along the bottom and reached it within a few minutes.

The cave was set about ten feet in from the rest of the solid rock, being situated in the middle of what looked to be a collapsed lower section of the wall. This created a rock shelter with an overhang, protecting the cave entrance from direct exposure to the elements. In fact, it almost looked like until the rock collapse, the cave may have been completely sealed off. Justus climbed from the bottom of the ravine to the rock platform about seven feet above the level of the brook. As it was past mid-afternoon, the sun was not providing direct sunlight into the crack of the gorge, but there was enough ambient light for Justus to enter the cave.

Upon crossing its threshold, Justus found himself in a roughly circular room about twenty feet in diameter. The light was adequate enough for him to see that the room was bare, save for occasional rock debris. However, once his eyes adjusted, a dark rectangle emerged on the opposite wall. Walking toward the shaded end of the room, he noticed that the rectangle was actually a door made of thick wooden planks made rough by the years. The door had no handle and was covered in ancient runic characters, which were unintelligible to him. He made several unsuccessful attempts at opening it, feeling frustrated that he couldn't explore further.

Seeing that no progress was to be made with the door and that the afternoon was drawing toward evening, Justus decided to return to the brook. He scoured the surrounding wall looking for a mode of ascent that wouldn't require him to retrace his steps and soon found that he could egress the gorge by stabilizing himself with trees on a series of switchbacks up to the top.

Cresting the top of the ravine, he found himself much closer to his house than he had anticipated. In fact, he was only several hundred yards away. Making a mental note of the location, he headed back to the house.

Once home, he found that Anna was up, although still looking sickly, and was preparing herself for dinner. Once served, she made a poor show of eating, but she made an effort to stomach as much as she could in her nauseous state. Justus finished his dinner and headed back to the bedroom with his wife.

"I know that it's still early," Anna began, "but I'm feeling pretty tired. I don't want you hanging around the 'sick room' while I sleep, so why don't you just come to bed whenever you're ready. In fact, you may want to give me as much space as possible until I'm feeling better. I wouldn't want to give you what I have, in case it's contagious."

"I'll probably hang out in the library again. I just can't get enough of exploring the books. There's so much in there that it would probably take me months to catalogue everything. I really hope that resting today helps you feel better tomorrow." He made a half turn as if to walk away, then turned back toward Anna. "By the way, I climbed down into that gorge from the bridge this afternoon and found an interesting little cave with a locked door in it after following the brook for a while. It's actually not far from the house."

"You'll have to show me when I'm feeling better. I'd like to do some more exploring around the area. But that will have to be for another day. I need to rest now. I love you. Goodnight."

"Goodnight, honey. I love you too." With that, Justus headed again for the library.

It was still early in the evening, so he made a pretense of canvassing the bookshelves in the unique room, but his mind kept returning to the book that he had begun reading on the two previous nights. Finally, he gave in to the compulsion, climbed the ladder, and found the book back in its original place. He was stymied in his attempts to account for how the book had been returned to its spot on the bookshelf, so he just grabbed the book, descended the ladder, and assumed the place of reading that had become familiar to him the last two nights. Justus settled in to a comfortable position and began to read.

* * *

The hunting dogs that had been running among the horses, weaving in and out between their feet, were now nowhere to be seen, but their constant barking gave a clear signal that the hunters could follow. Once the dogs smelled out their quarry, the men would spring into action and the hunt would be on. Indeed, it was less than ten minutes before the constant, measured barking of the dogs turned into the frenzied, high-pitched baying of a bloodthirsty dog on the trail of his prey.

The riders spurred their horses into action, galloping through the woods after the dogs. Justus followed Logan closely through the gloom of the morning, racing against the other hunters to secure the hunted and win the prize offered by their lord.

The barking, which had been growing more faint, suddenly began growing much louder, indicating that the group of deer had reversed direction in their panic and were headed toward the riders. The deer veered again to the right of Justus and Logan, who swerved after the chase. They had been on the left flank of the riders, so they were riding hard, pressing their mounts to catch up with the rest of their group. This was tricky work, as the forest presented the challenges of low branches, fallen trees, and limited visibility.

They were gaining on the rest when a cheer arose from several of the men.

"Methinks an arrow has pierced a deer. Let us ride to see," Logan predicted.

His forecast proved to be correct, as the baying dogs and riders had gathered in a small clearing in the woods at the base of a small, but rocky, summit. A wounded deer was caught amongst a semi-circular cropping of rock, the snarling dogs, and the menacing hunters.

"'Tis mine arrow has pierced this stag, and 'twill be mine that ends its life."

Justus recognized Bana as the speaker, the dangerous looking knight who arrived with Logan the day that Justus was tested by Lord Alden. Logan and Justus entered the clearing a moment after the rest of the party, in time to watch Bana dismount and walk slowly toward the wounded deer.

"Fool," Justus heard Logan mutter under his breath. "Like a peacock on display he struts. He is contented not with the life of the beast; he must put on a show as well."

Bana slowly approached the injured animal, bleeding at the base of the arrow protruding from its haunches. He pulled an arrow from his quiver and expertly notched it on the string. He took a few more steps toward the beast, wanting his quarry to know the victor. Raising his bow, he was just at the moment of release when a commotion near the edge of the clearing grabbed the group's attention. One of the dogs had separated from the party and was chasing a squealing baby boar out of the brush and into the clearing.

The unexpected squeals of the boar distracted the dogs and spooked the horses. Chaos reigned as the dogs chased the new game, running under hoof, further disrupting the horses. The deer saw its opportunity and darted away into the thicket on the other side of the clearing. Before the men could control their horses and regain the chase, a giant, snarling she-boar tore into the clearing and headed toward the most obvious target, Bana.

Bana's rushed bow shot was off the mark, merely grazing the bristly flank of the crazed, charging beast. Any thought of making another attempt was swept aside as the ravening boar quickly closed the distance. Bana turned in desperation to find some foothold on the rock surface.

As if in slow motion, Justus saw the scene develop, and he knew almost instinctively when the boar first crashed through the underbrush that Bana's life was in danger. Being behind the rest of the hunters, his horse was sheltered from the spectacle of the dog chasing the wild piglet and the ensuing chaos. Maintaining control of his mount, he quickly spurred his horse into the center of the enclosure, angling toward the boar while the rest of the group looked on helplessly.

Approaching the boar from its left side, Justus pulled his horse alongside the charging swine and leaped onto its back, his hunting knife flashing in the air. He plunged the knife into the thick shoulder of the beast and attempted to remain on its back. However, the impact of his leap, and the blade in its shoulder caused the boar to stumble full career, sending Justus tumbling across the turf directly in front of it.

Kicking wildly to regain its footing, the boar fixed its beady eyes on Justus, aiming to gore him with its tusks. Having quickly regained his feet, Justus assumed a defensive position, hoping his instinct and training would help him stay alive. As Justus braced for impact, the boar suddenly thrust its head sideways and downward into the dirt, grinding to a halt, twitching spasmodically at Justus' feet. A hunting spear was still wobbling slowly back and forth from the powerful thrust that brained the wild boar. Justus looked up to see Lord Alden dismounting his steed to recover his spear.

"Better weapons are there to bring down a boar than a hunting knife," Lord Alden proclaimed for all to hear. The obvious pride on his face made it clear that his words were no rebuke. He placed his foot on the boar's head and plucked out his spear with a mighty pull. He then yanked the hunting knife out of the boar, cleaned it off in the grass, and handed it back to Justus. Lord Alden picked two men out of the group to help Justus and Logan clean the boar and transport the giant beast back to the stronghold. "The rest of us shall track the wounded stag and see if there is more game to be had!"

Bana left the rock escarpment with a look of shame and anger darkening his countenance. He walked past Justus without a word and quickly remounted his horse. He followed behind Lord Alden, as the rest of the men followed their liege out of the clearing and after the baying dogs.

Justus still had not moved from his position when Logan clapped him on the back and said, "You could well have chosen a less perilous way to win the approval of your lord."

"I wasn't looking for approval," Justus countered. "Bana was in danger, and I was the only one able to help. It just kind of happened without even thinking."

"Sir Bana," Logan replied.

"What?" Justus asked, somewhat confused by the reply.

"You have acquitted yourself well in this hunt and have earned a place as a warrior in your lord's hall. From this point forward, you must render proper courtesies to those superior to you. Sir Bana is a knight and must be called 'Sir.'"

"Right. *Sir* Bana was in danger."

"Yes, that he was. Little do you know it, but you have advanced much in our lord's eyes on this morn. Skill with a weapon can be taught, but bravery is a measure of a warrior, and you must have it in abundance to attack a she-boar with naught but a knife. Brave...else you are a mad fool!" he declared with a chuckle, again slapping Justus happily on the back.

The men quickly set to work cleaning the boar and creating a makeshift stretcher upon which they could drag the animal back. The stretcher was strapped to Logan's horse, and the other two men rode about fifty paces ahead of Logan and Justus on the ride back to the settlment. The first half of the ride was in silence until Justus asked a question that had been plaguing him since the hunters left the clearing.

"Logan…Sir, Logan, I mean. I noticed that Sir Bana looked angry after he walked past me toward his horse. I would think having his life saved should be enough to make him grateful."

"Ah, Sir Bana. There is not much to know about him, save two things. He is an esteemed warrior, and he is proud. In saving his life, you have humbled him. You are no knight, yet your bravery and quick action made him seem the fool in his own eyes. How quickly the peacock strut was turned to fear," Logan mused with a chuckle. "You did no wrong, rather his pride was brought low. You will also be highly esteemed by Lord Alden at his expense, which maddens him even more. Worry not. You are a favorite now."

Despite Logan's assurances, Justus was disturbed by Sir Bana's behavior. He didn't trust him and decided to be cautious, avoiding him whenever possible.

They soon arrived back at the holding, bringing the swine into the settlement. They collected many curious onlookers, with Logan and the other two hunters spreading the tale of the morning's hunt. Logan and Justus proceeded to Lord Alden's hall for some refreshment and to wait until the rest of the hunting party returned.

In fact, it was not long in coming. They easily tracked down the wounded deer, finding that the dogs had finished the job that Bana started, but demonstrated their good training by not ripping open the flesh of the deer and spoiling the meat. Once dressed, the deer was strapped on the back of a horse and Lord Alden declared an end to the hunt. The boar would provide more than enough meat for a feast, and the events in the clearing had allowed the remaining deer to make good their escape, so there was no trace of any other game when tracking the wounded deer. Lord Alden was more than happy to head back to his hall to spread the news of the exciting hunt.

That night, a blazing fire lit Lord Alden's hall, and the smell of roasting pig filled the nostrils of its occupants. Dripping fat sizzled in the fire as the haunches of the boar were turned on the spit. Warriors and women filled the hall, with dogs waiting along the walls for scraps to be thrown to them.

The roasted pig was served to the cheerful men and women, along with bread, cheese, and drink. After consuming his fill, Lord Alden stood and called the room to attention.

"Knights, warriors, and ladies, on this very morn I took leave to enjoin the ancient sport of the hunt. I did promise a new spear to the man who slayed the biggest stag. This honor belongs to Sir Bana, whom we can thank for filling our bellies with venison." Lord Alden signaled a servant boy, who brought forward a thick war spear, its iron head polished to a shine, reflecting smartly in the firelight.

Bana stood and received the spear with a reluctant smile on his face and returned to his seat amidst a smattering of cheers from the feasters.

"However…," Lord Alden bellowed in a loud voice to regain the attention of the revelers. "However, the slaying of a stag was not the sole excitement of the hunt this day. One of my best knights lives to receive his spear because of the quick actions of another. Justus, I ask you to stand."

The surprise was evident on Justus' face as he stood at his place next to Logan. Dogs whining impatiently were the only sound in the room as the people awaited the words of their liege.

"This day Justus has earned a place among my warriors with his actions and bravery. He did forsake concern of life and limb and slew the boar with naught but his hunting knife."

The men and women erupted in cheers. The deeds of men are greater in their halls than they were in battle, and this occasion was no exception. The resounding acceptance of the tale was not diminished in the eyes of the listeners with its departure from the truth. It was understood among the men and women of the hall that deeds of bravery and valor should be made greater upon each retelling, and the exaggeration of their lord showed his pride in Justus' actions.

When the cheers began to die down, Lord Alden continued. "Justus did not do this without help, though. One steed managed to keep composure and rushed to enjoin battle with the boar. We owe Justus our thanks for this feast and for the life of Sir Bana. Therefore, unto Justus I give the mount upon which he rode. Without them both, I fear tonight would be one of mourning and not celebration."

Cheers arose again as Justus stood with all eyes upon him. One pair of eyes, however, robbed Justus of his enjoyment of the moment. There was a darkness in Sir Bana's eyes as he sat glowering at his place at the table. Justus uncomfortably averted his gaze as the cheers continued.

6

The Knighting of Justus

The next day Justus awoke fresh and ready to continue his training with Sir Logan. He arose just before dawn and headed to the stables to see his prize. Justus stood and watched his horse stamp idly in the stables and marveled at the powerful, regal creature. The horse was tall and strong, but not thick. It was fleet of foot and had great endurance. The months of riding had produced a mutual respect between horse and rider, and the bay colored horse nuzzled Justus as he approached. Justus understood that a horse was a rare and expensive gift, and could still hardly believe his fortunes when Sir Logan approached him from behind.

"Our lord is generous, is he not?" Sir Logan mused.

"I should say so. This was completely unexpected. I didn't even kill the boar."

"Hearken to my words from yester morn. Did I not say that valor and honor characterize knighthood? What you did in the face of danger and death to save a knight was the very stuff of valor and honor. You did place yourself in grave danger for another, and did it more swiftly than any other present. Lord Alden has been pleased with you, and your actions have demonstrated your qualities. Have you named your steed?"

"He's a bay horse, so I was thinking of calling him Bayard."

"'Tis a worthy name. Bayard it is," affirmed Sir Logan with a smile. "I hope you are ready to continue your training. Now that you can lay claim to the title 'warrior', you must be prepared to do your lord's bidding. Come, let us to the lists and test your skill with the joust."

Justus and Sir Logan readied their horses and dressed themselves with mail and plate armor. Once readied, they secured two lances each and headed to opposite ends of the lists. One lance was placed upright in a wooden cylinder for ease of retrieval, should a lance break. The other was held by the jousters.

"When one of us does break both lances, we shall see who has had the better of this tilt!" Sir Logan called from his end. They couched their lances and steadied their horses. "Ready…Charge!!"

On the command, Justus and Sir Logan spurred their horses to speed. They steadied their lances and braced for impact, both of them bursting their lances on each other's shield but remaining horsed. They rode to the end of the lists, both grabbed a new lance and charged again.

Sweat was beginning to run down Justus' face inside his helmet. He tried to blink the sweat away, but the stinging salt blurred his vision. Distracted by the stinging in his eyes, he was not quite prepared for impact, and his lance glanced weakly off Sir Logan's shield, while Sir Logan's lance caught Justus off guard, knocking him back from his saddle and onto Bayard's haunches. He bounced awkwardly for a stride or two before falling backward off the horse.

Sir Logan's laugh carried across the tilt yard as Justus picked himself up from the ground and removed his helmet. He quickly wiped the sweat from his eyes and retrieved Bayard.

"I see that only your pride is injured," said Sir Logan once he had his laughter under control. "All those hours at quintain has served you well, although you do need more than a glancing blow to unseat the likes of me."

"Well, I guess I've got some more work to do before I'm the one who's laughing."

* * *

The rest of the day and, indeed, the next several months passed as they had for

Justus, training to hone his skills as a warrior. Slowly, his muscles hardened, his sword quickened, his horsemanship excelled, his arrows flew true, and his confidence improved. Without Justus' knowledge, Sir Logan was making regular reports to Lord Alden on the progress of his pupil, until the time was ready for Justus to prove himself in battle.

Lord Alden spread word throughout the fort that he was to have a counsel that evening with all of his household warriors and the knights who served him. There was no immediate word of its purpose, but smoke rising from a village in the distance seemed a likely topic. Sir Logan caught up with Justus an hour prior to the meeting to speak with him.

"'Tis likely our lord does call us hence to a council for battle. More like than not, we shall ride upon the morn and seek those who pillage and destroy upon the lands of our liege. Forsooth, we will find out tonight.

"Be not afraid for what the morrow brings. Forget not your training, and you will acquit yourself well upon the field of battle. Many untested warriors succumb to fear before their first test, but once the conflict is upon you, there is no room for fear."

Soon the men were all gathered in Lord Alden's hall to hear what news he brought them. The room was strangely silent, as there were no children or women found within the walls this night. The only noises were from the few dogs shuffling around, making themselves comfortable.

Lord Alden's voice finally broke the silence, "Men, I call you together this night to ensure swift retribution on our enemies. The cries of innocent people did ascend to heaven in smoke at dawn on this very morn. Riders in black have brought death to mine lands, and I will have justice. Before the sun has surmounted the horizon on the morrow, we shall be at the ready to do battle. I know this be the work of that devil, Prince Broga. Long has he used lawlessness to undermine his brother, the king. His hand is in this, mark my word. Twenty warriors shall remain here to safeguard the women and children. Twenty shall accompany five knights and me to right this wrong. Ready yourselves, men. We ride at dawn!"

He quickly made the assignments among his warriors, so each knew who would stay and who would go. Justus thought he detected a faint smile of pride on Lord Alden's face when he chose him to accompany the warriors going to battle. The company dispersed at Lord Alden's word, and they readied themselves for the morning's rendezvous. It was determined that Sir Bana would remain and guard the settlement in Lord Alden's absence. Justus searched for Sir Logan to discuss what he could expect in the morning. However, he went to bed without satisfaction, discovering that Sir Logan had departed to exercise his horse on a ride.

It was before dawn when the twenty-six men were present to depart. Lord Alden was arrayed in polished, plate armor on his upper body, which hid much of the chain mail that was underneath. His polished metal greaves and gauntlets had whorls of gold etched in them, and his helmet boasted a silver circlet. His silver eagle crest adorned his shield, its wings spread wide, a sword clutched in its talons. Lord Alden's horse was arrayed in the finery of war, a thick red cloth encasing the body of the horse, showing beneath protective metal plates.

The knights were arrayed similarly, if not as spectacularly. To protect their torsos, they all wore metal plates on top of chain mail that protected their arms and upper legs. Each wore greaves, gauntlets, and helmets as well. Each of their horses wore protective gear, and the knights were each afforded their sword, shield, and a lance.

The warriors were arrayed more simply. They could afford no plated armor, but each was protected by mail, greaves, gauntlets, and helmets that covered only the tops of their heads. Their shields were larger than those of the knights, and they were also afforded a sword and a sturdy spear. Although the warriors fought on foot, they rode palfreys, protected only by hardened leather, to ensure swiftness in gaining their location.

They rode quietly through the fading darkness following the lines of smoke ascending from the burned villages. Justus and Logan were assigned to the rear guard of the party, and they spoke quietly about the battle to come.

"What are we up against today?" asked Justus, hoping he didn't sound as nervous as he felt.

"Our lord suspects the hand of Prince Broga in this. He is the eldest brother of our king, Geraint. Their father, king before Geraint, imprisoned the crown prince for a year and a day for the grievous slaying of a minor noble, who had unwittingly crossed Prince Broga. The old king fell ill and died while the prince was still imprisoned, and the laws of primogeniture were broken, as no man serving punishment for murder may be crowned king. Thus good Prince Geraint was rightly crowned king. Upon his release, Prince Broga, his soul is as black as his armor, made an ill-advised attempt upon the crown. The terms of his surrender were to be forever banished from the capital city, and he was removed to an estate in a distant area of the kingdom. Since his banishment, he has harried the people and has worked to subtly undermine his brother. His power has been growing as of late, as has his boldness. However, the fox is sly and takes care to disavow any wrongdoing, and he is never directly involved in carrying out the destruction.

"Not all lords are created the same. Some have vast wealth and command castles and armies, inherited from nobility throughout their generations. Others are made lords by the king, through noble actions or prowess and bravery in battle. Lord Alden is such a lord. Born of humble servants, Lord Alden distinguished himself in the service of King Geraint and was knighted. He did not see wealth or warriors as a thing to be grasped, rather repeatedly yielded them in the service to his king. Accordingly, years of faithful and generous service were rewarded with a title and a goodly tract of land. Thus, Lord Alden is newly made, not born, into lordship, hence the wooden palisades and not a sturdy curtain wall of stone. The faithfulness of Lord Alden to his king has created enmity between himself and the black Prince Broga. The prince would not risk a direct assault, but, from time to time, there have been suspicious attacks led on our liege's land. That, Justus, is what we ride into, a feud that runs deep. We will likely face a band of marauding knights only bent on evil. Lord Alden's band is small, but he must protect his lands from the villain prince."

Sir Logan ceased speaking when he noticed the men slowing down as they entered a clearing. Inside the clearing was a smattering of mud huts with thatched roofs and livestock milling about in the muddy enclosures. Dogs barked as more of the men rode out of the woods. The riders passed a lame, old man sitting on the outskirts of the little village muttering to himself, his saliva dripping onto the mud that caked his beard. He lifted his gaunt head up as the men rode past, but his eyes remained unfocused, like he couldn't see what was happening in front of him. He continued to mutter to himself and lowered his head again before all the men had passed, as if he had lost interest in the procession. Justus looked back to see the man covered in dirt, sitting in the mud, rags covering loose leather-like skin over bone.

He barely had time to feel pity for the man before Lord Alden called the men to a halt. He ordered a villager over who had emerged from his hut to silence his barking dog and bade him rouse the village and evacuate into the woods. Lord Alden wanted the area clear of peasant targets when the battle was enjoined. With the help of five warriors deployed to evacuate the village, all was empty within thirty minutes. Once accomplished, the men did not have long to wait before the pounding of approaching hooves indicated that a sentry was rushing with some news.

"My lord, I see black riders not more than three miles to the east. It seems they hasten in this direction."

"How many?" was all that Lord Alden asked.

"Lord, I counted ten knights in full battle gear. They have no warriors in their company. They attack quickly and escape quickly."

"Knights, warriors, listen to me. We have but moments before battle will be enjoined. There is glory and honor to be found this day. Bring honor to God, bring honor to your lord, bring honor to your fellows in arms, and bring honor to yourself!

"Warriors, place yourselves in a two-deep shield wall between the rogue knights and the village. Knights, split in two groups and conceal yourselves behind huts on either edge of the village. When the black knights attack the shield wall, fly from behind the huts and attack their flanks. Now go, and Godspeed to victory."

The warriors quickly formed a line with Lord Alden at the center and the knights dispersed behind the huts at either end of the village. Lord Alden positioned Justus next to him in the front line, the men standing side by side with their shields interlocked, the men in front with swords in hand and the men in the rear line with long spears.

As the sun rose above the horizon and flooded the valley with light, the men shifted anxiously, the minutes seeming like hours. Most of Lord Alden's men were battle tested and brave, but each knew the destruction that a mounted knight could inflict on unmounted warriors. Despite their superior numbers, a well-trained, mounted knight was worth any number of warriors, and the number of knights counted by the sentry was more than the number of knights who rode with Lord Alden.

In reality, the men had been in place and waiting less than ten minutes before the first black knight broke through the edge of the forest and headed toward the village, followed by more knights in his retinue. But much to the dismay of Lord Alden and his men, another group of knights broke from the forest to the west of the first line of knights. The two clusters of enemies rode toward each other at an angle, forming a flying wedge to break through the wall of warriors, hoping to destroy the small force and burn down the village.

Justus had numbered the charging knights at twenty when the implications of the tactics of the charge struck him, and he leaned in toward Lord Alden, "We have been betrayed, lord. They must have known we were going to be here and the size of our force to attack us like this. They knew what they would be facing before they left the wood line."

"It pains me, but I do think the same. We are not prepared to face such a force. I fear for the worst."

"My lord, allow me to step forward and face the oncomers before they reach the line."

"Do not be a fool, death is all that awaits you that way," Lord Alden replied.

"Lord, death is all that awaits me here if I stay. Allow me to face them, and we may yet come through."

Lord Alden hesitated, and that was all the permission Justus needed. He stepped from the line, which quickly closed behind him, and he ran toward the oncoming wedge of charging knights.

The knights were closing quickly, and Justus sprinted from the line of warriors toward them. He stopped about thirty yards in front of his companions and waited in a defensive posture, shield raised in his left hand

and sword hoisted in his right.

In the final seconds before impact, time seemed to stretch itself out in front of him. He could see the black shields with silver bossing around the edges bounce up and down with the rhythm of the horses. He could see clods of turf fly into the air behind the horses as they careered down the sides of the valley toward the village. The flanks of the horses heaved with exertion and were flecked with foam. The lead knight seemed to be in slow motion as he raised his lance with his right hand and steadied it against his shield, aiming directly at Justus' torso.

The distance between the wedge of knights and Justus had closed to less than twenty feet when he suddenly did a half-pirouette to his left, went down on one knee, and ducked his head. He simultaneously flung back both of his arms, striking the nose of the lead horse with the flat of his blade with such force that it's head was forced back and to its right, causing it to stumble into the horse following closely behind in the wedge. Justus had positioned his grip on his shield in such a way that when he swung his left hand back, he sent the shield hurtling like a disc, shattering the front leg of the horse leading the other side of the charge. The horse went head-first into the turf, launching its rider into the path of the knights on the same side of the formation.

The lead horse veering to its right and the downed horse on its left caused the formation to erupt into chaos. The knights on the left side of the wedge tried desperately to avoid the thrown knight, only succeeding in entangling themselves with each other, knocking their lances askew. The lead horse continued to veer to its right, causing a domino effect on the knights on the right side of the wedge. Each of the knights attempted to slow his horse quickly to avoid running into each successive rider. The resulting confusion culminated in several more thrown knights and a complete disruption of the formation.

The broken wedge had carried past Justus, and he quickly stood and engaged the black knights. He succeeded in pulling several more knights from their horses in the confusion, quickly dispatching them. Only thirteen of the original twenty knights remained horsed, but their confusion was such that they were easily overwhelmed by Lord Alden's warriors and the knights, who had emerged from behind the huts.

None of the black knights escaped or yielded. Even those who were disarmed chose death over submitting to Lord Alden, and none would part with any information regarding who had sent them killing and burning. Only one of the charging horses had been wounded, which was shortly put down, the wound caused by Justus' hurtling shield. None of Lord Alden's men had been lost.

The men stripped the fallen knights of their armor, weapons, and other valuables and loaded the plunder on the remaining horses. They gathered the bodies away from the village and burned them, sparing the villagers from the gruesome work of dealing with the dead. Once the fire had taken and was sending flames high into the air, Lord Alden sent two riders to gather the villagers from the woods and bring them back to their homes. Before the remaining group departed, Lord Alden called them to attention.

"Goodly knights and warriors, hearken to my voice! This day, we have seen a wondrous act of bravery on this field of battle that did save our lives and the lives of these humble peasants. Not one of our lives is lost, and our enemies are routed. This noble deed must needs be rewarded, although no material reward will suffice. Therefore, will it please Justus to step forward."

Justus left the line of men and stood facing Lord Alden. He felt like butterflies were jostling about in his stomach, as he was unsure about being singled out from among his brothers in arms. He had expected no rewards or accolades for his actions. Rather, he was fighting for the preservation of his life and the men with him.

"Justus," Lord Alden's voice pulled Justus' attention back to his liege, "have you bowed to the lordship of the Christ, the Son of God?"

"Yes, I have, lord," Justus answered.

"Do you solemnly swear to uphold justice, to fight for the good of Christendom, and to accept no one into knighthood who does not swear to do so?"

"I do, lord."

"Then kneel before me."

Although an inkling of what was about to happen had snuck into his mind, it was all happening so quickly that it didn't seem real. Nonetheless, Justus took to one knee before his lord and bowed his head. Lord Alden drew his sword and tapped both of Justus' shoulders with the flat.

"I dub you Sir Justus. Stand and present yourself to your fellows."

7

Darkness Descends

Justus rode in the place of honor with his lord on the journey home, and Lord Alden spoke more to him on this occasion than during the previous months he had been training with Sir Logan.

"That was a goodly display. 'Tis a rare gift of bravery and swiftness of thought you have. It will serve you well in your career as a knight."

"Lord, I was just trying to avoid a slaughter. It was more good fortune than anything," Justus replied.

"Nonsense!" Lord Alden said with vehemence. Then with a softer voice, "Do not sell your gifts short. Every man there desired to avoid slaughter. Yet one man turned that slaughter upon its head - just one man. Humility is necessary, but one must be able to accept praise. You have much skill and 'twas developed very quickly. Your potential has not yet been met, true, but accept credit where it is due."

"Yes, my lord," was all Justus replied.

Sensing that Sir Justus was still coming to grips with his new found fortunes, Lord Alden continued his discourse to ease the burden of conversation for Justus.

"'Tis the duty of every knight to first serve the Christ and then to serve his liege. Serve both well, and you will have a goodly life.

"I was not always a lord. I advanced through faithful service, as can you. I serve my lord, King Geraint, faithfully, and he has rewarded me with title and lands. I foresee great things for you, from which I would not hold you back. I believe that you would best be served in the employ of the king. I have been watching you ever since your arrival, and I have been much impressed. Your skills overmatch any glory you might win with me, and you may win much renown in the service of the king. I would still be your lord, but I would be rendering service to my lord in loaning you to him. Serve him well, and you will be much rewarded. You shall depart on the morrow to join the king. Much you have to discuss, I am sure, so you may ride with your teacher for the remainder of the journey." Lord Alden's pride was obvious, as he reached over and patted Bayard's neck and called up several warriors to give them instructions concerning Justus' journey the next day.

Justus dropped back to ride with Sir Logan to discuss his swift change in fortunes.

"I'm leaving tomorrow," he opened sullenly. "I haven't even finished my training."

"Nay, my work with you is complete. There is naught that I can teach you that experience will not. My days as your teacher are done. 'Twould not be proper for a knight to instruct a brother knight. Nay, your schooling is over..." his voice trailed off betraying his disappointment as well.

"What do you think will happen with me?"

"That part is no mystery. You will accompany your escort into the presence of the king, and you will serve at his pleasure.

"Lord Alden sees much in you, and rightly, and has decided that keeping you here is as much a disservice to himself as to you."

"I don't know that I follow," Justus interjected.

Sir Logan smiled sadly before answering. "A knight cannot surpass his lord. Therefore, you are limited by the successes or failures of Lord Alden. He knows this and sees better for you. Sending you to the king increases your fortunes and Lord Alden's. Sending a goodly knight to the king will ensure future considerations for Lord Alden. The more honor you do win, the greater the considerations for our lord, whether it be in more lands, a better title, or a handsome payment to secure your release from Lord Alden.

He is working in his best interests, yes, but in yours also. You may not see it now, but he is rewarding you. You did save his life and those of his men. He would have been either ruined or dead, were it not for your swift actions. 'Tis for the best, yet I will miss you."

"I'm sure we'll see each other again, though. Won't we?" concern creeping into Justus' voice.

"To be sure, to be sure. Lord Alden and his men not infrequently ride in the service of the king. Be not afraid, Sir Justus. You go on to better things. Think of your old teacher when you have made a name for yourself in this world." A broad smile crossed Sir Logan's face with those words, and Justus smiled in return, feeling more comfortable at Sir Logan's confidence. They rode in silence for the rest of the short journey and came into view of the wooden palisades before noon.

Even from a distance, the men could tell that someone had arrived during their departure. The small community was bustling, and a score of extra horses were being fed near the stables by a groom. The palfreys were richly attired in black leather with their riders nowhere to be seen.

Lord Alden quickly called over several grooms to attend to their horses, and he led his men immediately into his hall. There he found a score of lightly armed emissaries from Prince Broga talking quietly with Sir Bana, who quickly cut off conversation and called attention to his approaching lord.

"Lord Scand, to what do I owe this dubious honor?" the loathing obvious in Lord Alden's voice.

"I did hear that you were out for a ride on this beauteous morn. I hope you did fare well," replied Prince Broga's principal advisor and most powerful noble.

"I did fare better than your black prince's minions who have been burning and killing on my lands. My lord king will not stand for this flagrant breach of honor. Tell your prince that his fate will be the same as his men whose blood now soaks my soil." The anger flashed in Lord Alden's eyes, but he dared not kill a prince's emissary in his own hall unprovoked, vile though they may be.

"My prince disavows any knowledge of marauders in your lands," Lord Scand replied mechanically, as if the lines were so well rehearsed, they lost any meaning to him. "But that is not why we are here. My prince seeks to remedy the schism between him and some of the nobles of the land who have misinterpreted his loyalty to his brother. He sends us to issue an invitation to you to accept hospitality in his hall one week hence. What say you?"

"You can tell your *prince* that there has been no misinterpretation. I will reach no accord with him," he said with a snarl.

"Such is what I feared," replied Lord Scand unconcernedly. "Very well, men, let us not tarry. We will receive a better reception elsewhere." Without a word, the men left the hall, mounted their horses, and rode out of the settlement.

"Those vile blackguards think they will treaty with me!" Lord Alden shouted after the riders had left. "I will have naught to do with them and their murderous prince. To the Devil with him!" and he stormed out of the hall, leaving the men standing in silence.

The onlookers slowly dispersed to care for their horses and the plunder that was taken. Justus took special care in grooming Bayard, as he would be riding him into battle from now on as a knight, and he would be doing it in the service of the king. The thought of leaving tomorrow made him both sad and anxious. He would miss Sir Logan and Lord Alden, and he was unsure what his future now held. He still felt like a stranger, despite his nearly one year tenure with them. He didn't share their culture or their history; he was just inexplicably thrown in with them and had to learn his way as he went along.

It was the middle of the afternoon when he had finished with Bayard and made his way to the hall to look for Sir Logan. A short distance from his destination, he heard voices coming from inside. The voices were low, but it was clear that the conversation was strained. Justus recognized the voices of Lord Alden and Sir Bana.

"But lord, how could it have been me?" protested Sir Bana. "I was with you the whole time during the preparations, and my wife can attest to my presence during the night."

"But we were betrayed!" the emotions fraying Lord Alden's voice. "The black riders knew we were coming and how to meet us. How did they know?!"

"Lord, I know not of which you speak. I am not guilty of this."

"What were you and Lord Scand discussing when I arrived?" Lord Alden asked suspiciously.

"Lord, you did leave me in your stead during your absence. I was acting in that capacity when you arrived. They were merely relaying their message. There was no need to continue with me upon your arrival, thus they dispatched their message to you. They came after your departure, lord, and could in no way have influenced what happened in battle."

"I know," Lord Alden said, frustration and weariness weighing heavy in his voice. "There is a traitor in our midst, and he must be found out."

"Lord, if I may point something out…," Sir Bana began.

"Yes."

"Far be it from me to make accusations, but was it not Sir Logan who went riding yester evening? Were not all the men making preparations for the morn when Sir Logan asked his leave? Were the men not in their beds with their wives, with no one to account for Sir Logan's whereabouts? Lord, a traitor there is, and Sir Logan is he!"

Justus started back when he heard the accusation. He had never trusted Sir Bana, and he could not accept the explanation. However, he couldn't find fault in the logic. Sir Logan was the only one who asked leave last night. The other men made their preparations and turned in with their families. On the surface, Sir Bana did not appear to be implicated, and things looked poorly for Sir Logan. Justus' thoughts were interrupted by a command from Lord Alden.

"Bring him to me. Find him and bring him to me. He may struggle if he knows he is found out. Take ten men, and bind him if you must, but bring him to me! By the Rood, I will not countenance traitors!"

When Justus understood what lay in store for Sir Logan, he knew he needed to warn him. He felt sure that Sir Logan was innocent of the charge, but doubt had begun its work and was fraying the edges of his confidence in his friend. After a quick scan of the camp, Sir Logan was nowhere to be found, so Justus quickly crept away from the hall before Sir Bana could find him eavesdropping.

He was well away from when he heard Sir Bana call for the household warriors and send word through the camp of Sir Logan's treachery. Justus ran to the stables, saddled his horse, slung a shield on his back, grabbed his sword and scabbard, and rode for the woods. He had left the settlement behind before the hue and cry had sufficiently caught hold and was headed for the stream several miles away, where he knew Sir Logan loved to while away his free time.

Justus arrived at the spot about fifteen minutes later to find it bereft of any sign of Sir Logan. He spent the next half an hour searching the woods for his friend but to no avail. He then rode into a nearby clearing, which was when he first noticed the smoke.

Thick, black smoke was billowing from the direction of Lord Alden's settlement. He spurred Bayard to speed in the direction of the smoke, riding furiously through the woods, the branches scratching at him as he rode. Foam was flecked on Bayard's flanks as he leapt small streams, fallen trees, and charged hard across open meadows.

After what seemed like an eternity of riding, Justus finally broke free from the last stretch of woods before the stronghold. The smell of the smoke and the heat of the fire accosted his senses, as he pushed Bayard even faster up the hill. It was clear that the central hall was fully engulfed in flames and that it was spreading to surrounding buildings. The screams of women and children filled the air, and terror filled Justus as he rode through the gates.

The screams quickly ended as the roof of the hall collapsed, spewing flames and sparks high into the air. Contrary to what he had expected, no one was moving about. Besides the flames and billowing smoke, it was eerily still in the stronghold. The flames continued to spread, the thatch of the roofs igniting like tinder, and the light breeze only sped up the destruction.

Justus knew that he did not have much time before the fire would engulf the whole compound. He dismounted Bayard, tethering him to a post away from the fire. He ran swiftly to the great hall only to have his worst fears realized.

It was clear that this is where the last stand took place. The bodies of Lord Alden's knights and household warriors lay cut down in front of the hall. Most of them didn't have weapons. The peasants, women, and children had been herded into the hall, apparently for their protection, but the burning of the hall and the subsequent roof collapse had silenced them forever.

Justus, cut with grief, looked for any survivors outside of the hall. He found none, but what he did find only intensified his grief. Lord Alden was found in a pool of his own blood, having been savagely cut down. Next to him he found Sir Bana, likewise cut down. Justus dropped to his knees next to Lord Alden. He wept openly for his lord, the one who took him in, fed him, trained him, believed in him, and knighted him. He owed much of what he had to Lord Alden, who was a kind and generous lord. Now he lay in his own offal, his life ingloriously snatched from him.

A ray of hope struck Justus that caused him to rise to his feet and recheck the slain bodies. The only one missing from Lord Alden's knights and warriors was Sir Logan. He must still be alive! As soon as the thought struck him, however, he realized the implication of what he had discovered. His mind replayed the conversation he had overheard between Lord Alden and Sir Bana, accusing Sir Logan of complicity with Prince Broga and his marauders. He had always distrusted Sir Bana, but now he had apparently fought to the death by the side of his lord. As most of the warriors were unarmed, the attack must have been a surprise and was likely led by one who was trusted. It seems that Sir Logan committed the ultimate act of betrayal, likely returning with Lord Scand and his men, only to utterly destroy the settlement.

Hurt beyond words by the betrayal of one that he loved and trusted, Justus let loose a scream of agony. The scream caused Bayard to rear back and whinny, drawing Justus' attention back to his horse and the immediate danger the fire was to both of them. Fighting off weakness in his knees, he made his way to his horse and rode out through the gates and away from the settlement. He spurred his horse to speed toward the woods.

He rode away from the fire, Lord Alden's settlement, and his past. There would be no more happy days with his lord and his friend. He would not be joining the service of the king the next day. He rode on aimlessly, mile after mile, mirroring how he now felt about his life. He knew no one; he had no place to stay. He only had Bayard, the clothes on his back, his shield, and his sword. He felt overwhelmed and at a loss to know what he should do next.

So, he rode. He rode until he was so exhausted that his slumped, grief-stricken form fell from the saddle in some nameless wood.

8

From Bad to Worse

Justus groggily wiped his eyes and peered around him. He had a difficult time placing himself in his surroundings. He sat bolt upright in momentary fear before he recognized his library.

Have I been dreaming so long that I didn't even recognize my own home? he thought. "That was the most incredible dream of my life. The detail…and it seemed like I was gone months," he said to himself. "I've never dreamt a storyline before," he realized. "My dreams now seem to pick up where the last one left off."

He stood up to leave the library and was just about to open the door when it flung open with Clive standing in the doorway.

"Sir, I believe that we must send for the doctor," concern thick in his voice.

"Why, what's the matter?" Justus replied beginning to feel panic rise up in him.

"She seems no better, sir. Indeed, she may have gotten worse overnight. I think the time to wait for improvement has passed. I believe medical consultation is needed."

Clive's assessment was indeed true, Anna lie in bed looking pale and weak. She mustered a smile when Justus entered the room. In just the few days that she had been feeling ill, it looked like she had lost weight and appeared that her skin was thinning out. Blue veins showed themselves under the surface that weren't visible before. She seemed lost in the covers on the bed, almost childlike in her helplessness.

"Maybe it's good that you haven't been sleeping with me at night. I wouldn't want you to come down with what I have," she said with as much smile as she could muster.

"Honey, don't talk too much. Clive is getting a doctor. We'll get you taken care of, and you'll feel better soon. I want you to just rest again today."

"I know you want me to rest," Anna replied, "but I've been in bed too long. I think a walk in the sunshine would do me some good. Would you mind walking with me outside for a little bit this morning?"

"Sure," Justus said, uncertainty creeping into his voice.

"Don't worry about me. I'm not so bad off that I can't go for a little walk. We probably have some time before the doctor comes. Let's go now."

Justus helped Anna out of bed and into clothes suitable for a morning walk. Blue sky greeted them as they exited their house. The green of the sylvan landscape and the lively chirping of birds stood in stark contrast to Anna's worsening condition. However, she was true to her word. Arm in arm, she walked with Justus in silence outside the house. The pace was leisurely to accommodate Anna's weakened state, nevertheless Justus noticed that her breathing was labored. He was immensely concerned about her health, but he knew the strength of spirit that Anna possessed, and she wouldn't want to dwell on her illness. As they drew near to the house, a car pulled down the lane and stopped in front. It was the doctor. Justus guided Anna back inside.

"Hello Anna, I'm Dr. Reuel. Let's have you sit down so I can take a look at you."

Dr. Reuel looked like he had come out of the late 19th century. He wore little wire rimmed glasses, a tweed jacket, and wool trousers. He had a full head of white hair that was partially matted, due to the derby that he had worn on the drive over. He had soft, but intense, blue eyes that seemed to notice nothing besides his patient. He opened his black leather bag, which was full of his medical instruments. He was in every way the prototypical doctor of yesteryear on a house call.

His manner seemed to put Anna at ease, and she relaxed under his grandfatherly touch. He rarely spoke other than uttering little assurances to his patient. He checked her pulse and blood pressure. He listened to her lungs and palpated her abdomen. He pulled out a needle, some tubing, and an empty vial. He used this to draw some of her blood for testing. When he had concluded his examination, he absentmindedly patted his pockets, as if he were looking for something.

"Ma'am, I'm hoping that the blood tests will shed light on this situation. Your heart rate is a little elevated and your blood pressure is a touch lower than normal, but your lungs are clear and you seem otherwise healthy. I'll get this sample to the laboratory today. Here is my card, should you need to get ahold of me in the meantime. There's nothing wrong with a little exercise, such as you took this morning, but rest should do you good. And don't forget to eat. You won't have any strength at all if you don't eat. I hope to be in contact in a few days with the results of the tests." He gave her a grandfatherly pat on the head and a genuine smile, then headed back out to the car.

"Now we wait," Justus said worriedly. "I can't stand waiting when it's something like this."

"It's okay, love," Anna replied. "We'll find out in a few days, they'll figure out what needs to be done, and we can put this all behind us. I think I'm feeling a little better from my walk anyway. I would like to lie down for a little while, though." Justus helped Anna to bed, tucked her in, and kissed her on the forehead.

"Don't worry too much about me. Try to stay busy and productive. It doesn't do anyone any good for both of us to be lying around the house."

"I'll do my best," he said, feeling more worried than he would like. He kissed Anna again, shut the door, and headed out into the hall.

Justus jumped back in surprise, as he ran into Clive, who was lurking nervously in the hallway.

"Can I help you with something?" Justus asked, probably sounding more annoyed than he meant.

"Actually, sir," came his reply, "That is exactly what I was going to ask you."

"I don't know," Justus replied distractedly. "I just need something to keep my mind occupied while we're just sitting around waiting."

"Whatever I can do to help."

Justus paused for a moment before he seemed to find some focus. "You know what? There is something that might keep me occupied for a little while. There's something I'd like to show you, see if you know anything about it. Follow me."

* * *

It wasn't long before Justus and Clive were picking their way down the ravine near the bridge. Justus had less time to concentrate on the beauty of the location, as he was hurrying along as fast as he could safely navigate without falling in the stream, and he was focused on his purpose of showing Clive the door.

It wasn't much longer when they turned the bend on the gorge near the waterfall, and the mouth of the cave opened before them. They climbed up to the landing in front of the cave, entered, and let their eyes adjust before stepping up to the mysterious wooden door.

"Strange, isn't it?" Justus mused, breaking the silence.

"Why yes, it is, sir…Most definitely strange." He stood silently, alternating between approaching the door and touching the runes or testing the strength of the wood and standing back with his arms crossed, his brow furrowed, deep in thought.

"You know," he continued after a lengthy silence, "it has been many years, and I thought it was just a wives' tale, but I have heard it said before that there was an ancient tomb roundabout this area. No one ever spoke of details, and I was never curious enough to explore much beyond the grounds of Ascalon Cottage. I wonder if this could be the grave of which they spoke."

"That would be interesting," Justus said, excited at the prospect, "and it looks pretty undisturbed. The only catch to that theory is that it appears locked…from the inside. I don't know that this would be a common practice for tombs."

"True," countered Clive, "but it could be just a security measure to keep unwanted intruders out, and they appear to have been successful."

Justus suddenly stepped forward to the door, "Clive, I just noticed that these characters here look different than the rest carved into the door." He pointed at characters carved about half way up the wooden slab. The rest of the script on the door was carven in long, slanting, elegant strokes. The ones to which Justus was pointing were made of rougher, shorter strokes and were carved in a small circle. He lightly traced the runes with his finger, testing their depth against the other, more graceful runes. Justus suddenly jumped back from the door with a gasp, leaving a small smudge of blood on the door. He clutched his right index finger and showed Clive the small laceration he had just received.

Within seconds, their attention was diverted from Justus' finger back to the door. The runic circle in the middle of the door was rotating, revealing something they had not noticed before – the circle was not part of the plank in which it was placed. Its rotation made visible the seam that marked it as a separate piece of wood. After one full rotation, a slight scraping noise and a muffled "clunk" came from somewhere inside or behind the door. At the "clunk", the door swung open just enough to let out a stream of cold, stale air.

"You might be right about the tomb idea," Justus said with a shiver, "that air makes me think of death."

"Nonetheless, you seem to have opened the door. The choice now lies before us. Do we enter or not?"

"I think this is too much to pass up, and if we find something interesting, maybe telling Anna about it will help distract her from feeling so sick. If you stay here, I'll run back to the house to get some flashlights. There's a way up near here that actually brings me up close to the house. It's a little steep to get down that way, but I'll be back as soon as I can."

"As you wish, sir. I shall but make myself comfortable until your return."

It was nearly half an hour before Justus returned with some flashlights and several lanterns in a backpack.

Justus stood for a moment to catch his breath before speaking. "I brought a couple of flashlights and lanterns. I brought the lanterns in case we want to light a few of them and set them around to add some ambient light once we get inside. Ready?"

"When you are, sir."

Justus pulled at the edge of the door and slowly opened it. He and Clive stood back, allowing the ancient air from behind the door to thoroughly mix with the fresh air from the outside. He handed a flashlight to Clive and took a deep breath.

"Well, here goes nothing," Justus declared and stepped inside.

Their flashlights sent focused beams that sliced the darkness. Both men stood in the doorway scouring the darkness in front of them, searching for any indications of danger. The flashlights revealed nothing but a tunnel that ran straight in front of them. The walls were cut out of the rock, and its smooth surface glistened with moisture. The ceiling was curved and high enough for both men to walk upright. It was not wide enough for them to walk abreast, so Justus took up his position in the front and proceeded slowly into the tunnel, with Clive right behind.

Justus then remembered the lanterns, lit two of them, and placed the flashlights in his backpack. The lanterns cast a dim light down the tunnel, which made the walls seem to glisten from the small droplets of water that were collecting on them. Now that the tunnel was illuminated, Justus and Clive started moving more quickly.

The tunnel ran about fifty feet in a strait line before turning ninety degrees to the right. A flight of stone steps started at the turn and descended a good fifteen feet below the level of the hallway. The air seemed closer at the bottom of the stairs and the walls covered with even more moisture. The stale air made breathing more difficult, but the men pressed on. They were quickly rewarded with another wooden door about twenty feet directly in front of the bottom step.

This time rust was working against them. The hinges of the ancient door were rusty and resistant to their attempts at opening it. They put their flashlights to good use, however, and used the end of them to knock so much rust off the hinges that they thought there would be nothing left of them. Their integrity was preserved well enough that the door slowly swung toward them with a loud groan of protest when Justus and Clive both pulled on the iron ring fastened to the door.

Involuntarily, they held their breath while the stale air from behind the door mixed with the air from the hallway. When Justus finally breathed again, the air around them seemed to stink of death even more. He shuddered before stepping to the threshold, telling himself that he was just cold.

Justus led the way into the room and was surprised to find that they no longer needed their lanterns to see, although they dared not put them out. Sconces placed on the wall of the circular room burned with small, reddish flames, giving the room an unnatural, amber hue. Justus imagined that this is what a world would look like that was lit by a dying red sun, so weak that most of its rays never penetrated the atmosphere.

The room was about twenty feet across and eight feet high and was cut out of the rock in the hillside. Beside the sconces, the only other item in the room was a sarcophagus placed on a low, circular stone dais in the center of the room.

A strange fear came over Justus when he saw the sarcophagus, but curiosity and the presence of Clive helped him quickly shake the feeling and move toward the interior of the room. Clive joined him in moving toward the stone coffin. They both held up their lanterns to add to the dim light of the room to see the sarcophagus better.

The thing itself was of exquisite beauty. It must have been created by an ancient Celtic master of stone work. A border of intricate Celtic knotwork was found on every slab. Each border was at least three inches wide and was filled with detailed lines that weaved and wound and turned back in on itself, displaying the mesmerizing form of a perfect Celtic knot. Inside the border the knotwork continued, but these lines created amazing and wonderful creatures, some real, some mythical, some unrecognizable and lost to a legendary past. Although each slab of the sarcophagus was unique and different, the knotwork inside the borders all joined in the middle to create a dragon encased in a circle. There was something familiar about the image, but he couldn't quite place it.

The intricacy and detail overawed Justus, "I can't imagine how long it took to create this. I've never seen anything like it."

"Nor have I, sir. This was clearly made for a prominent person," he replied, matching Justus' low whisper.

"What do we do now?" Justus continued, almost fearing to hear what Clive would say.

"Well, I suspect we open it. I shouldn't think we have come all this way to find the box only to return home and forget all about it."

"I was afraid you'd say that. I just have this strange, creepy feeling since we opened the door to this room. I can't quite explain it. Then again, I wouldn't be able to explain it if I came this far and just left it. I know you're right, I'm just a little creeped out. Plus, I've got a pretty good guess what we'll find in there."

"Right you are, but keep a stiff upper lip, and we'll get through the unpleasantries. I am sure your curiosity will get the better of you soon."

"There's no point in waiting, so give me a hand, Clive, and let's see what's in this thing. Be careful with the lid, though. I don't want this damaged."

Clive joined him, each grasping the sides of the sarcophagus lid at their respective ends. Fortunately, the lid was not more than an inch thick, and they managed to slide it off, set it down on the dais, and angle it against the side of the sarcophagus. Despite not being terribly thick, the exertion required to remove the lid was still significant, and both men were breathing heavily when they stood back up, beads of sweat forming on their foreheads.

A simultaneous gasp escaped their lips when Justus and Clive looked inside the coffin. True to their suspicions, a corpse lay inside. Upon closer inspection with their lanterns, it appeared to have been a woman. However, it was not the corpse that immediately caught their eye. Clasped upon her breast was the most beautiful sword they had ever seen. Its handle and hilt were made of intertwined silver and gold, with Celtic knotwork again represented. The knots spilled onto the steel blade and were etched down the center of the blade until they disappeared half way down. A perfect emerald was set in the pommel and brilliantly reflected even the low light cast from the lanterns. It was the most exquisite piece of art Justus had ever seen, and he stood entranced for several minutes before an awareness of the rest of the contents of the sarcophagus snapped him back to reality.

"It looks like a woman, Clive," was the only thing Justus could manage to say at that moment.

"Indeed. It looks like a woman not long enough dead as this woman should be."

Following Clive's lead, Justus took a closer look at the corpse. Where one would have expected just bones, or possibly leather-like skin draped over bones, if the body had been somehow well preserved over the centuries, the two men found that the corpse was readily recognizable as a woman. Her jet-black hair was fanned out underneath and above her head. Although her skin was ashen, thin, and dry, it gave the appearance of the remnants of flesh beneath it, like decay had not completely eradicated the last vestiges of muscle, fat, and connective tissue.

"She *is* remarkably well preserved. She looks to have been some sort of royalty, with the tomb, elaborate sarcophagus, and sword. I wonder if they used some special embalming technique to preserve her like this," Justus said with awe in his voice.

Clive did not reply immediately, as he continued to inspect the body. She wore a fine, silken black shirt underneath a black, hardened leather breastplate. A dragon was emblazoned in red across the leather and was partially covered by the sword. A skirt of sturdy, black material flowed out from underneath the breastplate. Her ashen skin stood in striking contrast to the black in which she was enshrouded.

Justus broke the silence, "I wonder what she looked like in life."

"I cannot say why, but I am glad I never knew. There seems something fierce about this one, even in death. Let us not further disturb the dead today. The day is drawing on, and I must begin preparations for supper."

Justus helped Clive replace the lid and followed him out of the tomb. Clive seemed to step faster and faster as he made his way through the tunnels, such that Justus had to fairly jog to keep up. When they finally broke into the sunshine, Clive seemed to breathe a sigh of relief and returned to a more sustainable pace.

"I'm glad you decided to slow down," joked Justus. "I thought you were trying to make me earn my supper."

"There is an unholy feeling about that place, and it was putting me in a state of discomfiture, what I believe you Americans call 'the willies.'"

Clive quickly became more relaxed as they made their way back home, and they spoke of nothing else besides what they had found.

9

A Realization

When Justus and Clive arrived back at the cottage, they found Anna sitting in the kitchen nibbling food.

"I thought I should probably eat something, and I wanted to make myself useful," her wan smile belying that she had not significantly improved. "Would you like to grab a bite to eat with me?"

Despite the fact that she was very obviously still feeling ill, it encouraged Justus to see her up and active, and the sun started to peak through the black cloud of his wife's illness. They had pleasant, if somewhat labored, conversation over dinner, and Anna didn't eat as much as Justus would have liked.

"If I get hungry later, I'll just get more to eat," Anna said in a comforting manner.

While Clive cleaned up after supper, Anna convinced Justus to go on another short walk with her outside. The walk did not last long, however, as Anna found herself tiring quickly, her heart pounding in her chest from the mild activity. They retired to the library, hoping to raise Anna's spirits with the incredible room.

Justus watched Anna closely as they sat in pleasant conversation on the couch. Although she tried to be light-hearted and quick with her responses, he noticed that significant conversation seemed to tax her. She would close her eyes and lean back against the couch periodically, seemingly regrouping. On occasion, she would get up and peruse a book or two before slumping back down on the couch. She eventually gave up the pretense of strength and lay in silence with her head in Justus' lap.

Within a quarter of an hour, Justus noticed the slow regular breathing of a peaceful sleep steal over Anna, and he was determined to just sit, stroking her beautiful dark hair as long as she remained asleep. Less than an hour later, Justus was startled awake from a doze that had crept over him by a scream.

Anna sat bolt upright, eyes wide with fright when Justus put his arm around her comfortingly and held her to him. Her breathing was quick and shallow, and he almost convinced himself that he could hear her heart beating, it was pounding so hard in her chest.

"What's the matter, honey? Was it a dream?"

She took a moment to compose herself before she replied, "It was just a dream, that's all. Just a dream. I was scared there for a minute, but I'm glad you're here with me. I don't remember much of the dream, but I remember a woman dressed all in black chasing me. I ran as fast as I could, but she was still gaining on me. The closer she got, the more scared I became. I screamed right before she could grab me, and I guess that's what woke me up."

"Woke both of us up," Justus said with a smile. "Why don't we turn in, get some good sleep, and see where things stand in the morning."

* * *

Justus awoke to the early morning sunlight, barely high enough to spill its rays over the window sill. He quickly looked over at Anna to see how she fared in the night, and only a glance was needed to show that she had quickly gotten worse. Her breathing was shallow and labored, her complexion grey. She still appeared to be sleeping, so Justus carefully got out of bed to find Clive. Predictably, he was already up and preparing breakfast in the kitchen.

"Clive, I don't know that we'll need breakfast this morning. We've got to get Anna to the hospital."

"How bad is it?" Clive replied, concern thick in his voice.

"I don't know, but it's a lot worse. It seems like it's work for her just to breathe. We've got to get her to the hospital quickly. I want her under medical observation."

The next hour was spent contacting the hospital, Dr. Reuel, and packing a few things for Anna. Clive put some food items in paper sacks for them to eat on the half an hour drive to the nearest hospital.

Dr. Reuel was there to meet them, and he was quickly convinced of the need for observation around the clock, given the precipitous decline of his patient. She was admitted immediately, and Dr. Reuel, Justus, and Clive helped Anna settle in as comfortably as possible.

Anna did not even make a show of protesting her hospital admission. She knew she was desperately ill, and her eyes belied her fears, even if her lips did not. The group spent the morning trying to support Anna and boost her morale, but the attention proved taxing to her. Ever sensitive to the condition of his patient, Dr. Reuel, dismissed Justus and Clive from the room so Anna could rest. He walked down the hospital corridor to relay instructions to the nursing staff before rejoining the men in the waiting room.

"She will be under constant observation by a well-trained medical staff. They will be running some tests on her, but mostly the best thing for her right now is rest. Please attempt to see her only during visitation hours and visits should be relatively short. Any stimulation seems to weary her at this point. I know you're worried, but try to keep yourself occupied. I'll make sure the staff keeps you updated on any changes."

Reluctantly, Justus agreed and he made the lonely drive home without his wife. Silence dominated in the car, and it seemed to take much longer than 30 minutes to get back. But half an hour after they departed the hospital, Clive was pulling back into the driveway at Ascalon Cottage. They ate a quick lunch, also in silence, before getting up and simultaneously heading to the library. They settled into chairs opposite one another, both seemingly having a difficult time knowing how to begin.

"I wish I knew what's going on with Anna. She was fine just a few days ago. How could she have gone downhill so fast? I'm retracing our steps in my mind to see if she ate something or was exposed to something that we don't know about." He ran his fingers through his hair in frustration. "She was fine the night I came into this library the first time to read, and she was sick the next morning. What happened that night?" Justus paused for a moment before saying, "The only thing that I know happened is she went to bed, and I started reading the book." His eyes widened in disbelief. "The book!"

Clive watched in confusion as Justus jumped from his seat, climbed a ladder and pulled an ancient volume from the shelf. Justus plopped the book down on the table and pointed to the knotwork and dragon on the cover of the book.

"I knew the design on the sarcophagus looked familiar! It's the same as the one on this book. How are these things connected?

"Speaking of connections," Justus continued thoughtfully, "Anna had a dream last night that was odd. She had fallen asleep with her head on my lap just on that couch over there," Justus said pointing to the couch, "and she woke up screaming. She said that a woman dressed all in black was chasing her and she screamed right before the woman caught her, which woke her up. What are the odds that she dreamed of a woman all in black when we just uncovered a female corpse dressed completely in black. I don't know where it all leads, but it seems too coincidental to me."

"You mentioned odd dreams that you've been having. Did these start with the reading of the book?"

"They did. I don't know how they're connected, but this must all be tied together somehow."

"That is an odd coincidence, sir," Clive began. "On the very same day, too…," his voice trailed off to silence. "These dreams of yours, what are they like, and can you control what you do in them?"

"They're just incredible. I'm in a medieval world, where I was taken in by a nobleman, fought in battles, earned my knighthood…" He paused for a moment, sadness creeping into his voice as he continued, "In my last dream, my only real friend there betrayed the nobleman and all who followed him to their deaths, I was the only one to escape. As far as controlling things in my dream, it seems like it," Justus replied. "They seem so real that I could swear that I'm actually there. So I would say, yeah, I think I have some control over what I do. But how does that help?"

"Well sir, it seems that these dreams are related to your reading and what is happening with your wife. Either that or it is an incredible coincidence. The best that I can offer you is to suggest that you look for connections in your next dream. You may find out something valuable - how these things are connected and what to do about it."

After a moment's pause, he began again. "There is nothing that I can do in your dreams, but that does not make me useless while you're awake. Let us investigate this woman in black further. Although it chills me to consider it, I suggest we return to the tomb immediately and see if we have not missed something that might prove useful."

They set off at once, taking no leisurely pace. They made good time and soon found themselves pausing to recover their breath in front of the cave. It suddenly struck Justus what an odd juxtaposition that was presented to him. As he stood on the rock, he looked at the lively stream, jumping down the waterfall, feeding the small plants along its edge with life-giving moisture. The sun shone down, blessing the ravine with light and life, creating an altogether pleasant scene. Behind him loomed the cave, dank and cold and lifeless. Darkness and death were inside, while light and life were outside. Yet love and duty toward his wife called him into the darkness. He felt fortunate to have Clive by his side to aid him in this unpleasant endeavor.

Having recovered sufficiently to continue, they lit their lanterns and proceeded to the interior of the cave, past the rune-covered door and into the long, dark tunnels. Quickly they made their way to the final door, the one that guarded the corpse.

They entered without pausing and walked slowly around the outside of the room in opposite directions, lanterns in hand looking for any clues. They met at the far end of the room, across from the door. Their careful search of the walls revealed nothing new. They continued their circuit of the room, this time focusing on the ceiling. They met again by the door, having learned nothing about the room that they had not discovered the day before. Scouring the floor for clues, they met again and were disappointed. At last, there was no choice but to do the very thing that they most dreaded. They would have to examine the corpse more closely. Placing several lanterns on the floor to illuminate the room, they grabbed the last two to help them with their examination.

As if on some predetermined cue, they stepped up on the dais on opposite ends of the sarcophagus and placed their hands on the lid. Pausing for a moment to gather their courage, Justus and Clive slid the lid off and placed it carefully on the floor. With some reluctance, Justus picked up his lantern and illuminated the body.

Cold dread passed through him, and he stood as if frozen, gaping at what he saw. Had Clive not interjected, Justus may have recovered his wits much more slowly.

"I can in no way account for what I see. It is beyond explanation, and is the last thing I would have expected to discover here today."

"What does this mean, Clive?" Justus asked, his voice quivering with emotion.

What they saw in the sarcophagus cowed any immediate response from Clive. The corpse, who the day before looked like a well-preserved noblewoman from antiquity now looked like someone who had just recently passed into the realms of the dead. Although the pallor of death was still present, her flesh looked whole and supple. Flesh had covered bone, tightening the skin, renewing the beauty this woman had once possessed. Her high forehead and cheekbones were complimented by the graceful form of her face. Her lips were full, yet firm, even in death. If it were not for the color of death upon her skin, Justus felt like her long, dark eyelashes might flutter at any moment, opening to reveal eyes as dark as the night. Her features were alluringly feminine, yet hard, as if this was a woman who had commanded men.

"Let us go," Clive's words causing Justus to jump, "There is nothing we can discuss here that we cannot in the comfort and safety of the cottage, and the sooner we have departed this unholy place, the better."

The men replaced the sarcophagus lid, and quickly picked up their belongings, fairly running from the cave. They had put a good distance between them and their discovery before either one of them felt at ease enough to finish the journey at a walk.

* * *

They had been sitting in the library for nearly thirty minutes before either of them had recovered enough to speak.

Finally, Justus broke the silence, "Clive, what was *that?*" his voice a mixture of concern, fear, and bewilderment.

"That, sir, was a body that has no business looking like it does, and, forgive me for saying so, looks like it is only one step removed from re-animation. I cannot but think that it is somehow related to everything that has gone on, although what it means I do not know."

"I am afraid you may be right, but what scares me the most is that I feel like I am a helpless pawn in some terrible game that I can't figure out, and if I lose the game, then I lose my wife."

"I have that same fear, sir."

"What do we do then? I'm at a loss right now, and I can't take this feeling of helplessness."

"Sir, I fear that there is no more that we can do today other than what I have already suggested. There may be answers in your dreams, if now you look for them. You must continue to read at night. This may be the only way in which an answer is presented to you."

Justus knew that Clive was right, but he hated the feeling of impotence that accompanied his wife lying sick in the hospital. The afternoon slowly turned into evening, seemingly stretching on for days, despite Clive's best efforts to keep Justus occupied. The late supper seemed like it would never come, but Justus eventually found himself seated in the kitchen with Clive, nervously nibbling at the food set before him. Finishing his meal half-heartedly, he got up and began pacing about the house. Clive perceived that in Justus' agitated state, it was probably best to leave him alone with his thoughts.

As the evening drew on and the moon established its dominance in the night sky, Justus found that he had restricted his pacing to the area around the library, like he was waiting for some magic time of night when he should enter and begin reading. Before he entered the library, however, he found Clive and gave him a few last instructions.

"Clive, I'm about to go into the library for the night. Most other nights I've slept in the library, someone woke me up in the morning, so I'm liable to be asleep in there all night. If I haven't come out of the library in the morning and you have news of Anna, please wake me up. Say a prayer for me tonight, Clive. I really hope this works. I don't know what to do otherwise."

"We may yet have some time, sir. See where your dreams take you tonight, and we will talk in the morning. Good night, sir."

"Good night, Clive."

With that, Justus left him and hurried to the library. He quickly pulled the book down from its place and settled into his chair. He took a few deep breaths, uttered a short but desperate prayer for the health of his wife, and began reading.

10

In the House of the Hermit

Justus slipped seamlessly between waking and dreaming, the usual clear distinction between the two blurring to create a tormenting pseudo-reality that he felt like he could not escape. This continued for days until he finally awoke with a scream, sitting bolt upright. His heavy breathing was the only sound he heard, his sweat sticking to his clammy skin. After several minutes, his breathing slowed and he was able to take stock of his surroundings. He was in a small, simple room that smelled of damp earth. He was on a crude bed of rushes that appeared to be fresh, save for where his sweat had soaked. Nearby was a small, wooden table of simple make. A solitary candle burned near an urn filled with water. Some of the walls appeared to be cut out of the earth, while others were of wood, plain but sturdily made.

Suddenly, he heard another noise. It was a male voice singing in some other darkened room. A dancing light could be seen coming toward the room in which Justus found himself. A sudden fear gripped him, and he vainly looked for his sword. He soon found that his fear was misplaced, as a pleasant looking, ancient man stepped into the room holding a candle. He was dressed in a faded blue robe with a white rope tied around his waist, and his feet were shod in fraying sandals. His face was weather worn and wrinkled by the years. A shock of unruly white hair crowned his head. His grey eyes were friendly but full of wisdom. Despite the obvious appearance of age, he was unstooped and appeared more hale than his thin frame would suggest.

"Ah, thou dost awake from thy slumber, I see," said the hermit in a friendly tone. "I heard ye waken and bethought strange environs would nae set ye at ease. I am called 'the hermit o' the greenwood' by the commoners, but having been mine guest for this fortnight, ye may call me Sientio." His face turned eager for a moment, "Ye have heard of the famous Sir Sientio, have ye not?"

"No, I have not," was all Justus could reply before regressing back into confused silence. Numerous thoughts flashed through his mind in an instant, from concerns about his safety, to the whereabouts of his weapons and horse, to the identity of the aged man, to the shock of hearing that he had been bedridden for two weeks.

The child-like eagerness quickly left the hermit's face, which seemed to suffer from a passing sadness before he spoke again, "'Twas long years past," he said as if lost in a memory. "No, of course ye have nae heard of such a knight, for he no longer exists." A sad smile played on the corner of his lips before he took a deep breath and started again.

"Sientio is my name, and that ye may call me. I am the hermit o' these woods, and my days are spent serving my Lord and rendering what service I may to those who pass through. I have learnt some about ye by thy feverish speech these last weeks, but I know not thy name and how much of those words I may believe." He pulled up a plain stool next to the bed and sat down.

"My name is Sir Justus, and that only recently, although 'Sorrow' would be a better name for me."

"Aye, thy speech was filled with such talk. Such loss ye hath faced to be a fortnight abed with a sickness o' the soul. 'Twas no physical malady what kept you low. Ah, but I am sure ye are wondering how ye came to be in my care.

"Well, that is a story short enough. I found ye fallen to the turf, still as death ye were. Death 'twas my fear as well, until I noticed thy breathing. A countenance cold and pale I beheld and knew you to be needing the help of the Lord's humble servant. 'Tis a good horse of thine. He didst keep watch over ye and was standing right whence ye were found. Worry not," Sientio quickly added when he saw concern flash across Justus' face, "thy steed hast been well looked after and may be a bit plumper for it all when ye take thy leave. Thy weapons, Sir Justus, have also been under mine care."

"I don't know how to thank you," Justus said with sincere appreciation.

"Oh, no thanks are needed when the work is for the Lord, but all debts would be clear if ye would light the candle on your mystery. 'Tis naught but darkness for me now."

"I'll tell you my sorrow," the pain was thick in Justus' voice. "My best friend and teacher has betrayed my lord to death, has destroyed all he had, and I am in exile."

Sientio played with the ends of his beard, leaning forward in genuine interest. "Aye, 'tis a tale of woe, tell on."

"I learned the craft of war in the house of Lord Alden. He took me in when I had nothing and saw something in me that I didn't see myself. He gave me the chance and allowed me to study under Sir Logan, his best knight. I was knighted after my first battle, and I was to enter into the service of King Geraint. I never got that chance, though. Sir Logan killed Lord Alden, destroyed his home, slaughtered his warriors, and scattered abroad those he was protecting. I only survived, because I was looking for Sir Logan, which led me away from the stronghold. When I saw the destruction, I fled, and I don't remember much beyond that."

"The darkness of thy mystery deepens with the telling. I perceive there is more untold than has been told. What is yet hidden must be the candle to light this darkness. Tell me, what profit is there for Sir Logan in unseating his lord?"

"I've been trying to figure that out. If anyone was a traitor, I would have figured it to be Sir Bana, another of Lord Alden's knights. I never liked the look of him, and I don't think he liked me much either. Just prior to the betrayal, an emissary of Prince Broga, Lord Scand, came to invite Lord Alden to a council, but Lord Alden rejected the offer. Then I overheard Sir Bana accusing Sir Logan before Lord Alden. That's when I rode to warn Sir Logan about his danger. I did not find him before I noticed the smoke from the burning of the settlement. I arrived to find all dead, including Sir Bana at Lord Alden's side. My lord was dead, my friend a traitor, and I now had no one to recommend me to the king. So I fled. I didn't know where I was going, and in truth, I must have been half mad."

"Forsooth, half mad ye were, but ye faculties hath returned. Aye, Lord Alden was a goodly lord. Mine heart is saddened to hear of his demise. Would that some of the others ye have mentioned were in his place.

"Many years have I in this realm," he continued. "'Twas a lifetime ago, it seems, that a knight was I in the service of the king. Not Geraint, mind ye, but his father, King Tilian. Much worship did I win in his service." A distant, melancholy look suffused Sientio's eyes as he spoke, as if a sad longing for days gone by filled his heart. "Tilian was a goodly king, and well were his knights rewarded. Much renown and wealth were to be had in those days, and both were mine in double portion. Alas, but pride can bring one low, and such is the penance I must serve." He seemed to snap out of the sad reverie with those words and continued.

"But I speak not to talk of my tale, but of what concerns ye. Two sons had King Tilian, prince Geraint and prince Broga. From the days of their youth, one was comely and fair, strong and brave. The other was of a different ilk. He was scheming and brooding and dark. A malcontent he was. Many a gray hair on the good king's head could thank that rascal Prince Broga. Broga was the elder and in line for king, but his wiles were only held in check by periodic confinement. Upon the death of the good king, the coronation was held to proclaim Prince Geraint king.

King Geraint trod in the steps of his father, bringing prosperity to his people. However, peace evaded him through the schemes of his brother. Fear of death was always on his doorstep, but death was no master of him. No, a brave man was he and no fool. His brother was well watched." Sientio leaned forward and lowered his voice, as if he was afraid what he was about to say would be overheard. "No, 'twas nae his brother that he learned to fear. 'Twas his brother's wife!" A look of anger crossed his face as he continued. "Black is the heart of that woman, and evil drives her ambition. Oh, beauty hath she like none other, but a dragon she is underneath. A wretched worm and witch she is! Hate and substance she adds to her prince's malcontent. She is the one to fear. Aye, she is the one to fear." Sientio lapsed into silence, prompting Justus to speak.

"So how does this help me? I don't quite understand what I should learn from the history you've given me."

"Are ye still blind to what has transpired? Alas that I should live to see this day. I know not what hope remains, but hope we may trust while good yet survives. Sir Justus, 'tis my fear that the life of the king may be forfeit, if it is not lost already. It seems that Prince Broga has come to collect what he sees as his due. Where we find faithful lords laid low, we will find the king a close quarry."

Justus was stunned, sat upright in bed and swung his legs over the edge, as if preparing to leap out of bed into the fight. "You mean that the king could be dead? What of the other lords and the knights in his service? Could they not protect him?"

"Many seasons have I seen come and go since the Black Prince didst begin plotting his way to the crown. More likely is he now to succeed with his treacherous wife."

"I need to do something. Although my lord is dead, my king is not, and I owe him my service. I must leave in the morning, as soon as the sun is up."

"I fear ye be right," stated Sientio gravely. "May caution by thy friend, as I cannae offer ye protection beyond the walls of mine home. In the meantime, take what rest ye may this night. I will wake thee in the morn, return to thee what is thine, and ensure ye art provisioned well. Sleep ye well," he concluded as he stood and left Justus to himself. The shadows spread around the room as the comforting light of the candle left with the hermit, and the blackness of fear and doubt surrounded Justus.

* * *

Dawn awoke to find Justus and Sientio gathering provisions for the journey. While Justus saddled his horse and gathered what few personal items he had with him, Sientio was packing copious amounts of provisions into saddle bags he was giving to Justus for the journey.

"Thank you for what you've done. You saved my life," said Justus, as he warmly clasped the hermit's hands.

"Thy thanks are welcomed, but thy life may yet need saving. 'Tis no easy thing ye are set out to do. I pray ye eat well for a day or two to gather thy strength. Ye will nae run low on food for at least a fortnight. May God bless ye with good fortune."

"Where should I go if I want to best help the king?" queried Justus.

"Mine heart tells me that it matters not. Forsooth, the king's enemies may be all about by now. Trust to the Lord's leading, and you will not stray."

Justus mounted Bayard and turned his horse to leave before quickly turning to face Sientio to ask one final question, "How will I know her when I see her, Prince Broga's wife?"

"No description will ye need. Ye will know her upon sight. But to ease thy mind, I will tell ye quick. Hair as black as a raven…skin as fine as ivory… beauty surpassed by none. Guard thy soul well, and be not ensnared by her charms." A look of sadness mingled with regret changed his countenance as he concluded, "Her name is Lady Draic." With his head hanging down, he lapsed into silence.

"Thank you, and God's blessings on you. I hope to be able to repay you someday." With that, Justus spurred his horse to speed.

* * *

A blanket of stars looked down on Justus as he slept. The hard-ridden miles of the day slowly eased from his muscles, as sleep gave him a reprieve from his worries. His riding had given him no further direction, no clue upon which he could focus his energies. He felt just as lost at nightfall as he did at sunup, but now he was alone. Sleep took all of this from him, at least until the morning sun peeking over the tree line woke him from his peaceful, dreamless slumber.

Justus ate a filling breakfast from the provisions Sientio had given him. He was feeling the effects of two weeks of illness and inactivity. As quickly as possible he wanted to regain his strength and avoid the all too frequent breaks that were required had been required today. He hoped that eating well for a few days would strengthen him, as Sientio had suggested.

Bayard bore him for several uneventful hours before Justus entered a small glade. The clearing burst upon him from the thick trees through which he had been riding. The change was so sudden that Justus had to shield his eyes from the glaring sun no longer blocked by the trees.

"Halt!" a harsh voice came ringing out from the clearing. Justus' eyes had not yet adjusted to the brilliance of the sun, and he could not see who was issuing the command. He quickly pulled Bayard up to a stop.

"Declare your name and your purpose!" the voice challenged.

"My name is Sir Justus, and I am a knight-errant. It is purpose that I seek."

"Sir Justus, is it?" continued the harsh voice. "An ill-made knight you are wandering with naught but a sword and shield. Have you no armor, knight?" As Justus' eyes adjusted he began to see a group of knights at the far edge of the clearing with the speaker challenging him from a horse about twenty paces in front of his men.

"No, I don't. Not anymore."

"Then you must do without. I care not for the presentation of my foes, just for their defeat. As you have no lance, I challenge you to hand to hand combat." The knight rode slowly toward the center of the clearing and stopped to wait for Justus' response. His men followed at a distance and fanned out behind him, still on horseback.

As a knight, Justus had no choice but to accept. His slow ride to the center of the clearing was tacit acceptance of the challenge. As he rode, he scanned his opponent and the group of knights for any distinctive markings. The men wore polished armor with plain helmets. No feature set any one apart from another, with the exception of Justus' challenger. A grey cape was draped across his shoulders and down his back, and a grey plume crested his helmet.

Disdain leaked from the knight's voice as Justus approached, "I am the Grey Knight and am lord of these lands. You have no leave to cross here, and you will pay for your trespass with your death or with your servitude."

Justus dismounted Bayard and approached the Grey Knight with his shield up and sword in hand. The knight then dismounted and addressed Justus. "Let the fighting commence!" and he charged.

At a decided disadvantage, Justus chose to focus on defensive measures and judge the skill of his attacker. He hoped to either wear him down or take advantage of some mistake. The Grey Knight did not easily wear down, and Justus quickly realized that his strength had been sapped by his illness to a greater extent than he had anticipated. Even defensive measures were quickly tiring him, and he was lacking the speed and strength to take advantage of the mistakes. Despite his slowed and weakened state, he fought on doggedly, winning the admiration of his onlookers and raising the ire of his opponent.

After more than half an hour of exchanging blows, Justus' arms seemed to be leaden, and he was slowing significantly. Finally, a bone-shattering sword stroke fell upon Justus' shield, causing his fatigued arm to drop. A split second later, the Grey Knight rammed his shield into Justus' chest, knocking the wind out of him as he fell to his back. In an instant, the knight was upon him.

"Yield or die," he shouted triumphantly.

Anger and frustration welled up within Justus' chest, but he knew that yielding to this rogue knight was the only possibility for him to pursue Sir Logan and the Black Prince. He may even find direction while in the service of this lord.

"I yield," he said meekly.

"So my men can hear," the triumph obvious in his gloating voice.

"I yield!" replied Justus.

"Such is as I expected. Knights! tie the hands of this man, and we shall see how he does look being led like a dog back to his master's home." He laughed wickedly as his men obeyed. A knight quickly approached him and carefully tied his hands. Justus was surprised at the care with which this knight treated him. Another knight retrieved his sword and shield, and a third retrieved Bayard. So he walked. And he walked, and he walked until his feet were too heavy to lift. At last, when he felt he could no longer continue, they had reached the abode of the Grey Knight.

11

In the Abode of the Grey Knight

Justus was weak and sore when he arrived at his new home. When taken to his living quarters, he collapsed on his straw bed and slept like the dead all night. When he awoke, he was gripped by confusion and fear, which only abated as the memory of the previous day pushed away his mental fog.

The morning sunshine illuminated the room in which he had slept, revealing a barracks-like building that housed a dozen warriors on straw mattresses. The other warriors were already up for the day, but Justus quickly noticed a backlit form darkening the doorway.

"I see you have finally arisen," came the friendly voice from the man in the door.

"Yes, I'm awake, although I feel like I could sleep forever after yesterday."

"'Twas a hard day for you. The Grey Knight is a hard master for those who challenge him. Not all days will be as yesterday, but I think our lord has taken no liking to you.

"Sir, Justus, is it? 'Tis a rare knight that can challenge our lord thus, and I compliment you for your sword play. Alas, for you that you did not win." He paused for a moment before continuing, "Oh, our lord will not let you come to harm by *his* hands while you do serve him, but you have wounded his pride with the close battle yesterday, and you will not be his favorite.

"But shame on me for opining about your fortunes when introduction is lacking. I am Sir Nerian," he said as he stepped from the doorway into the room. "My family has served under the Grey Knight and his sires for generations. A prideful and vengeful lord is he, but he does share the plunder. So, worse lords there are to serve. I have been sent to see that you are acclimated and fit to battle as soon as you may."

"Well, I thank you for what kindness you can give me," said Justus, with lingering doubts about the situation in which he found himself. "I think food would go a long way to accomplishing our lord's desire for me."

"And food you shall have," Sir Nerian stated enthusiastically. "Come hence and we shall find you sustenance. Food would do me well too."

Justus followed Sir Nerian to the storehouses and breakfasted on apples, dry bread, and cheese. He was given water to wash it all down. The size of the storehouse led Justus to believe that the Grey Knight was a minor lord with small holdings. Given the confrontation yesterday, however, the Grey Knight probably commanded a more sizable group of knights than most of his peers, due to his mercenary activities and the resulting ability to pay them well.

Justus was then led to the armory and given a notched sword and a cracked shield. Besides a rusty mail shirt, he was given a leather jerkin and hard leather greaves and gauntlets.

"Where are my weapons and my horse?" demanded Justus.

"Your new lord lay claim to your goods. You do retain these replacement weapons at his pleasure. A horse will be given you at need…one that our lord deems suitable."

Impotent rage swelled in Justus' chest. He wanted to challenge the Grey Knight at full strength and make him beg for mercy, but he had yielded to him and owed him allegiance. Going back on that would be a loss of honor, which was unacceptable to all good knights. He would be forced to serve his new lord. Knowing this, despair soon replaced the rage, as he realized that the Black Prince could be running rampant throughout the country, with the King's life at stake.

"I know this news bodes not well for you, but you may one day win your lord's favor." After a short pause, silently acknowledging Justus' plight, he continued, "This day is one of rest for you. Our lord knows that you are no good to him sick or injured, but on the morrow you shalt enter his service fully, as have the rest of his knights. I will acquaint you with your environs, and then I recommend rest for you."

Sir Nerian spent the rest of the morning familiarizing Justus with his new home and lunched with him before sending him back to the barracks for rest.

As he lay on his bed of straw that evening, Justus alternated between seething anger and helplessness. He saw no way out and no appealing way forward. As emotional exhaustion crept over him, he took a deep, cleansing breath and silently mouthed a prayer to God to grant him aid during this difficult time. Even before he finished his prayer, his breathing became slow and regular, and he drifted off to sleep.

* * *

Early the next morning, he was awakened by Sir Nerian, "Sir Justus, sunrise calls, up with you to see what our lord wills."

Justus shook his head, as if he was shaking off the last bit of sleep, stood up and dressed for the day. He quickly broke his fast and was called to the presence of the Grey Knight within the hour.

Justus was escorted by Sir Nerian to their lord's hall. As he approached, Justus thought it lesser than Lord Alden's. It occurred to him that the goodness of his previous lord would improve any hall, but he found himself despising this one. Its doors were dark as he walked in. The only light inside came from several candles that were lit near the Grey Knight's seat. Curtains had been drawn over the windows, creating a dark and foreboding atmosphere.

"Ah, 'tis the mighty Sir Justus reporting to your new lord," he sneered. "To be sure, you will prove very useful to me. I see that you are hale and whole, so your work shall commence. I have ordered all knights and warriors under my command to deposit their swords, shields, and armor behind this hall.

'Tis time for the sharpening of swords and the polishing of armor. Two days hence, I will inspect your work, and, if it proves acceptable, you shall enjoy your next meal. You are dismissed to commence."

Justus was quickly led out the doors and behind the hall where it seemed like every weapon and piece of armor ever captured by the Grey Knight lay piled on the ground.

He knew that he was being singled out, and it made him furious. He also knew that his fury was impotent. As a knight, he could not soil his honor, and he also knew that his lord had the upper hand. His only chance was in making his fury work for him.

He quickly located a whetstone and rags for polishing. Justus went to work with a will and continued tirelessly throughout the day. When Sir Nerian came to bring him to bed, Justus refused. He continued working throughout the night, polishing armor and sharpening blade. By the time the first rays of the morning sun ushered out the darkness, Justus was putting the finishing touches on the last piece of armor.

Shortly thereafter, the Grey Knight appeared with several of his men to enjoy the sight of Justus struggling with the assigned task. He was shocked into silence seeing Justus standing proudly by the well-ordered pile of shining armor and the collection of swords and axes with sharp, gleaming blades.

Frustration showed on the face of the Grey Knight, and he quickly realized that he had lost this battle. Not wanting to lose face by showing emotion, he walked away without even completing the inspection.

Justus took his leave after his lord departed and quickly found Sir Nerian eating breakfast. Justus joined him and ate hungrily in silence.

"You are a fearless knight, Sir Justus."

"What do you mean?" replied Justus with a mouthful of bread.

"You do not play these games according to the rules of your lord. He does like to appear master in all circumstances, and it appears you do like to frustrate him in that."

"I did what he asked me to."

"That you did," Sir Nerian replied with a smile, letting the topic drop.

A few minutes later, Justus resumed conversation but in a different vein,

"I want to train. I want to get better at fighting, at shooting, at riding. Are there men here who will train with me?"

"There are men. Some may disdain you for your practice, but there are men. Often, our practice only comes when we are put to martial test on errands for our lord. Some foolishly exalt themselves thinking they need not practice. When would you start?"

"Today," Justus replied with a look of steely determination in his eyes.

"Not today, my friend. You are a determined knight and will no doubt win worship, but rest you need this day. And I need time to gather brother knights to practice. Take your rest, and on the morn we will commence."

After finishing breakfast, Justus took his leave of Sir Nerian and slowly walked the grounds, staying away from his lord's hall. The fury of yesterday had been replaced by cold determination. Rebelling against his lord and besmirching his honor was not an option, so he would become the best. He would win honor and wealth and perhaps buy his freedom. Weariness began to creep upon Justus after about an hour, and he walked back to his bed. He slept a refreshing, dreamless sleep through to the morning.

Justus awoke with the sun and found several fellow warriors awakening with him. One more was waiting outside with Sir Nerian.

"Sir Justus, 'tis no large number of knights were willing to cross blades with no wealth or honor at stake. These fellow knights are Gower, Arland, and Conall. Friends they are to me and friend they are to you. Let us commence, shall we?"

"Good to meet you," replied Justus gratefully. "I serve our master having been bested with a sword, so why not start there?"

The men all agreed, and the morning was spent roping off several sparring areas. A thick, wooden post was set up with a helmet placed atop, and a handful of branches, several inches thick and several feet long were gathered. The knights spent the day sparring with sticks and slashing at the post with their swords. They went about their training with energy and vigor, and their activities drew some stares, as servants and knights went about their daily routines. There was no sign of the Grey Knight that day, much to Justus' satisfaction. He desired no interference from his lord and wanted to train as often as possible.

The knights met again the next day and continued their swordplay. The second day's activities drew more attention, eliciting disdain from some and genuine interest from others. Again, their lord made no appearance anywhere near the training grounds.

On the third day of training, several more knights arrived early in the morning, looking to join in. They were welcomed heartily, and two more wooden posts were set up for training. The day's events proved an even bigger curiosity to passersby, as they noticed the new knights. Most passed by with interested glances, but this day some stopped and observed from time to time.

The practice continued every day, save the Sabbath, for several weeks. The ranks of the participants swelled to more than half the knights and household warriors who served the Grey Knight. Passersby now frequently stopped to admire the warriors and to cheer them on as they practiced swordplay, archery, and riding. Competitive, yet friendly games were set up to challenge the knights. At the end of each day, the knights supped heartily, laughed happily, and slept well. However, there were some who still scorned the knights, none more than Sir Camlin. He was a special favorite of the Grey Knight and was often found whispering in his ear.

One evening, after having observed the knights and warriors from a distance, Sir Camlin approached his lord, who was dining in his hall. "Oh generous lord, suffer me to bend your ear in private. I come with a pressing matter to discuss."

Despite showing his annoyance at having his supper interrupted, the Grey Knight sent his servants from the room. "What can you want badly enough to disturb my supper? And be quick."

"Lord, surely you know that a goodly portion of your knights and warriors do test each other daily at arms?"

"Yes, and what of it? Do you come to bear your jealousies to mine hall?"

"No lord, 'tis not me that my jealousies guard. 'Tis your interests alone that I seek to keep."

"And what interests of mine are hampered by yon knights?" sneered the

Grey Knight.

"Lord," Sir Camlin replied patiently, "I have been observing yon knights and warriors nigh daily for these past weeks, and what I have observed does cause me some concern. Lord, ever I work to expand your authority, yet it is my belief that your influence is being usurped."

"And how is this being accomplished, my faithful knight?" he added with sarcasm, still annoyed at having his supper interrupted.

"Lord, it is my belief that your newest knight, Sir Justus, has garnered significant influence with your men. He is tireless in his practice, he is generous with his words, and he is seen often full of mirth." Sir Camlin's lip curled in disgust as he spoke about Sir Justus, as if he was describing someone of despicable habits. "He is thick with your men. Many of them revere him, my lord. He is no favorite of yours, which makes his influence dangerous. Believe what you will, but he wields much power with those knights."

The Grey Knight's annoyance was replaced with attention, and he stopped chewing shortly after Sir Camlin began to describe Sir Justus' activities. Forgetting about his food, he focused on this new potential threat to his authority.

"What do you propose, Sir Camlin?"

"Lord, I believe that you must send him from here…"

The Grey Knight moved quickly to interject, but Sir Camlin continued, anticipating the protest. "Of course, I mean not to have you banish him. He is a knight of yours, and sending him away permanently might cause you to lose esteem with your men, and there is no predicting what Sir Justus may do if set free. There is no need to multiply enemies. Rather, send him on a quest – a difficult one. Send him poorly supplied. It may be that he never returns, not if you send a few of your most faithful knights to 'watch over' him on his quest." A gleam of hatred flickered in his eyes as he spoke the last sentence.

"You are a worthy knight, Sir Camlin, and I do have the remedy. Do you remember Lord Aelle? He did besmirch mine honor at our last meeting. That golden cup should have been mine! He was my last foe at the former tournament, as you may remember. How that fool was declared the victor is beyond reason. Methinks that the result was arranged. I will send Sir Justus to avenge my honor. I shall make it clear that any return without that cup will not be advantageous to him! Make the preparations and send three of my knights. I want him gone by morning!" With that, Sir Camlin strode from the hall and into the night.

12

Sir Justus' Quest

About an hour before sunrise, Justus was roughly awakened by Sir Camlin, "Sir Justus," he said in a harsh whisper, "our lord is in need of your services."

Justus dressed quickly and was ushered into the Grey Knight's hall. The hall was as Justus had first seen it, lit only by a few candles, whose poor light rendered the room gloomy. The Grey Knight sat in his chair on the dais at the end of the hall awaiting Justus' approach.

"Ah, Sir Justus, so good of you to come. I hope I did not disturb your slumber." He could not restrain a sly grin from crossing his face as he spoke.

"As you seem a most motivated knight, I require you to render your sworn services to me. Lord Aelle does live several scores of miles from these lands, and he did besmirch my person at our latest meeting. And he does possess something that I declare is not rightly his. You are to proceed as soon as you have been made ready and shall not return without this item, a certain golden chalice. You will know it by its design. 'Tis a plain golden cup, excepting the cross of our Lord in silver upon one side. A red ruby will be found at the head, foot, and two arms of the cross, symbolizing the blood of our Lord. I do not expect you to return without this cup. Fail me not in this!"

With those last words, several knights ushered Justus outside and back to the barracks to don his armor and retrieve his weapons. Justus still had the poor armor that was originally assigned to him. He had replaced the broken wood in the shield, but it was fit only for a squire at practice. His sword, though still notched, he had sharpened as best it could be. An old, sickly looking horse was given to him to ride. Anger burned inside of Justus at his predicament, but his rage was no longer impotent. He would face the challenge the best he could and trust to God for the rest.

"Where shall I find this Lord Aelle?" queried Justus from atop his mount.

"Ride east," laughed Sir Camlin. "You will find him eventually!" He smacked the rump of the horse, causing it to jump into an uncomfortable trot. The sight of Justus being jostled by the awkward gait of the horse brought the onlooking knights to derisive laughter.

Sir Camlin did not speak until Justus had ridden out of sight. "Yon three knights, saddle yourselves up and follow at a distance. Do nothing until the fate of his quest is sure. If he fails, we have no fear of his return. Should he, by some miracle, succeed, ensure that he returns not."

The knights shifted uncomfortably at their assignment. They took pleasure in the scorning of Sir Justus, but did not relish murder. Annoyance flashed across Sir Camlin's face at their hesitation.

"Do you not serve at your lord's command? Get you going and accomplish his wishes…and make haste!"

The knights quickly scampered off at being reminded of their position and duties. They suited up, gathered their weapons, mounted their horses, and slowly made for the place where Justus was last seen.

* * *

Justus had been riding as easterly as he could manage, setting himself toward the rising sun each morning, for four days with no incident. He had been given no provisions, so several hours each evening were spent foraging and hunting for anything he could get his hands on to eat. His mount ate grass freely at the frequent rests it required and drank greedily at the streams that watered the forests of the country. His horse ate and drank so well, in fact, that Justus noticed it required fewer breaks on the fourth day than on the

97

first. Despite still looking frail, it was holding its head more proudly and looking younger than before. Justus realized that the horse was not as old as it seemed, nor as sick – it was just poorly cared for.

Around noon on his fourth day of travel, Justus was approaching a clearing in the forest, when he heard raised voices a way off ahead of him. The voices became discernible as he paused just before entering the clearing.

"By the Rood, I shall have your heads, you miscreant knaves. Knights you are not, but murderers! A curse upon your families! Return mine horse and weapons to me before your honor is spotted yet further!"

Justus entered the clearing to see two warriors quickly leading a horse laden with supplies and weapons to a squire waiting near the edge of the forest, guarding their horses. The offended knight was on foot and without weapons, following the two thiefs. Another man was lying in the meadow, moaning, and attempting to drag himself toward the tree line.

Justus made for the squire at the edge of the forest as quickly as his horse could manage. The squire, also on horseback, had no armor, but was armed with a sword. He brandished his weapon as Justus approached, but his cowardice quickly surfaced, as he attempted to wheel his horse around and flee. However, in his panic, he forgot that he had the reins of the two warriors' horses wrapped around his hand. His attempts at turning failed, and he leapt in panic from his horse, still tethered to the mounts.

As Justus closed in on him, the squire dropped to his knees and begged for mercy. With a swift blow from the hilt of his sword, Justus knocked the squire unconscious, cut the tether cords, and scattered the riderless horses. The miscreant warriors espied Sir Justus' actions from a distance and sped up their pace, only to stop when they saw that quickly recovering their horses was impossible. One of these warriors then mounted the stolen horse and rode toward Justus. His partner then turned to challenge the aggrieved knight, who was still pursuing them.

Seeing his own disadvantage and that of the unarmed and horseless knight, Justus quickly angled his horse away from his attacker and galloped toward the second thieving warrior, who was still on foot.

Despite its weakened condition, Justus discovered that his horse was surprisingly swift, when pressed, and fearlessly charged at the knight. Not expecting to be challenged by the newcomer, the unmounted warrior turned too late to prevent being run down by Justus' horse. He was quickly overtaken and dispatched by the wronged knight, who had been following.

Justus turned his horse to join the pedestrian knight and placed himself about ten feet away, facing the oncoming attacker. Noticing that the assailing warrior on horseback was right handed, Justus placed himself on the left side of his companion, which would force the attacker to ride between them as he charged as Justus.

"Fellow knight, as he charges, slash at the horse's legs," Justus commanded his new ally.

There was no time for more direction, as the charging warrior arrived, brandishing his sword at Justus. Ignoring the knight on foot, he leaned to his right and aimed to strike a killing blow. But he never got the chance. His horse stumbled wildly at full career, throwing the attacker a good distance from Justus, who quickly dismounted to challenge him, if needed. As it turned out, no challenge was required. The villain lay lifeless in the grass, his head bent at an unnatural angle to the rest of his body. The badly injured horse was put down quickly and as humanely as possible, the knights lamenting the necessary evil.

"My eternal thanks to you, noble knight. What may I call you?" asked the grateful knight.

"My name is Sir Justus, and I am glad to have been of service."

"Sir Justus, your worshipful deeds have far surpassed what would be expected by looking at your steed and armor. How poorly outfitted is such a brave knight! My name is Sir Lorne, and this, my squire is…" Turning to introduce his squire, he remembered the injuries suffered at the hands of the murderous knights. He ran to him, with Justus following close behind.

The squire had not made it to the woods and was lying still in a pool of blood. His breaths came in shallow rasps as he lay dying in the meadow. He was weakening by the moment, and his deathly pallor and cold hands, which Sir Lorne was now grasping, announced that he would soon go the way of all men.

"Ah me," cried Sir Lorne. "Alas the day that I should see this. Good Anwell, beloved friend and faithful squire. Your end comes quickly and to my great grief." Tears fell from his eyes onto his dying friend, who could only manage a weak smile and a barely audible "Farewell, my friend." Anwell closed his eyes, and his life departed with one last rattling exhale.

"Go with God, good friend," Sir Lorne said quietly as he stood up and wiped his eyes. "'Tis a grievous loss for me…" He shook his head, as if to clear his thoughts of grief and addressed himself toward Sir Justus.

"I owe you my life, friend knight. How came you to happen upon my unhappy plight?"

"I am on a quest, Sir Lorne. I'm a knight in the service of the Grey Knight, and he's sent me to find Lord Aelle."

At the mention of the Grey Knight, Sir Lorne's countenance changed, and he withdrew a step from Justus. Sensing Sir Lorne's reaction, Justus quickly clarified.

"The Grey Knight is no friend of mine. Almost a month ago he bested me with the sword, and I yielded myself to him. In fact, I wouldn't be surprised if I'm on this quest so he can be rid of me for a while. I think he's trying to pick a fight with Lord Aelle and have me in the middle of it. I'm not exactly sure how I'm supposed to find him, so I need to worry about that before I figure out how to complete the quest."

A bright smile flashed across Sir Lorne's face, "I can help you with the first part of your quest and perhaps the second part as well. Come, I shall take you to Lord Aelle."

Justus helped transfer the knight's goods onto a new horse, they both mounted and readied themselves to ride, and Sir Lorne paused a moment, looking sadly upon his fallen friend.

"Anwell was an honorable man, a good squire and friend, and he did serve his lord well. Lord Aelle will send men to retrieve him and give him a Christian burial." He sighed heavily before continuing. "Well, let us be off."

The knights spurred their mounts and rode into the forest, covering the remaining distance to Lord Aelle's stronghold before nightfall.

As Justus and Sir Lorne approached the stronghold, they were greeted by sentries and allowed to pass at a word by Sir Lorne. Justus noticed the fine mail and weapons of the sentries as he rode by. They passed through two more groups of sentries before reaching the western gate of the large, wooden wall surrounding the compound. The wall, thickened by layers of wooden posts, was patrolled by men at arms, occupying a wooden walkway that circumnavigated the inside of the wall.

Upon entering the gate, Justus could see a large, busy stronghold of a motte-and-bailey construction. The large motte had been created with the earth dug from a trench around the outside of the wall. Upon the man-made hill was Lord Aelle's headquarters. The wall enclosed a large bailey, or courtyard, that surrounded the motte. It was to this motte that Sir Lorne was leading Justus.

Although the bailey was still bustling with activity, it was clear that the knights, men-at-arms, and peasants were winding down for the day. Only the armed sentries still maintained that sharp sense of purpose that would carry them through their nightly duties. The busyness of the men and women kept most of them from paying much attention to the newcomer.

Justus rode down the main thoroughfare that connected the west gate with the smaller, internal gate, allowing passage up the hill to Lord Aelle's hall. This gate was hung in a stone wall that stood about twenty paces from the base of the motte. Again, a word from Sir Lorne allowed passage, and they continued on the road up the hill.

Despite being man made, the hill was rather large, able to hold the lord's hall, dwellings for his servants, and several other buildings, serving as stables, granaries, armories, and his personal treasury.

Lord Aelle's hall was set toward the back of the motte and was large and stone-built, signifying the wealth of its lord. Thick, wooden doors, adorned with iron, barred the way from intruders, and three formidable men-at-arms stood sentry at the doors.

"I bring an honored guest to Lord Aelle's table this night," Sir Lorne announced.

The men-at-arms bowed their heads subserviently, and allowed the men to pass, opening the doors for them and shutting them behind. One of the men-at-arms entered as well to announce their coming.

Justus was immediately struck by the tasteful display of wealth inside the hall. Several large fireplaces provided light and warmth. Three large, candlelit, iron chandeliers hung in a line down the center of the hall. Rich tapestries provided color and insulation from the cold. Animal furs dotted the floors near seats and benches, to protect feet from the cold of the stone floors and to provide comfort. A large table was in the center of the hall, at which Lord Aelle and some of his knights were finishing their supper.

Before the guard took the opportunity to announce the knights, Sir Lorne spoke confidently, "My lord, it pleases me to accompany an honored guest to your hall."

Upon seeing the speaker, Lord Aelle, smiled broadly, "Have you returned so soon, my son?"

The shock of realizing who he had actually saved barely had time to register in Justus' mind before the conversation swung decidedly in his direction.

"Father, mine errand was foiled by two foul knights. My life was forfeit had not Sir Justus, this brave knight, come to my aid at the risk of his own harm. I tell you father, look not at this goodly knight's arms or dress. His value lies in the worship he did honorably earn through bravery and feat of arms."

At his father's encouragement, Sir Lorne recounted the story. Justus was abashed by the story he considered somewhat embellished, but Lord Aelle would hear none of his protestations. He rose from his place at the head of the table, approached the two knights, and merrily embraced them both. He ushered them to the table, dispatching servants to bring them food and drink. Upon returning to his place, his deep voice filled the hall.

"Let us raise the cup to this brave knight. To Sir Justus!"

The knights around the table stood and raised their cups in unison to the newcomer, crying out "To Sir Justus!" before swallowing a drink and returning to their seats. There was general clamor to hear the story again, which Sir Lorne was all too pleased to accommodate, much to the discomfort of Justus, who was not used to such attention.

As Lord Aelle's knights were finishing their supper, he soon dismissed them to discuss the events further with his son and Justus.

The great hall seemed very empty with just the three men, but Justus thought it no less pleasant. The cheerful fires and the chandeliers lit the hall well, and the furs and tapestries gave the hall a close, comfortable feel.

Lord Aelle retired to a seat near one of the fires with Justus and Sir Lorne following his lead. At his father's request, Sir Lorne again recounted the events of the day. Lord Aelle listened silently with a pleased smile on his face.

"…and thus I have brought him to you." This was stated to conclude Sir Lorne's story, but quickly his eyes widened as if remembering an important detail, and he continued, "I have just remembered that 'tis not only for honor did I bring Sir Justus to you. He did declare to me that it is upon a quest he does ride – a quest that was to bring him to you, dear father."

Lord Aelle raised an eyebrow in interest and beckoned Sir Justus to speak.

"Lord, what Sir Lorne says is true. I was sent to you by my lord, the Grey Knight…"

Lord Aelle leapt to his feet, anger flashing across his face, "What is the meaning of this," he bellowed, cutting off Justus' discourse.

Sensing the awkward situation in which Justus found himself, Sir Lorne intervened, "Father, pray let him continue."

Seeing that his son already knew more than he did, he returned to his seat and listened, although he was not so at ease as before.

"Lord, I am unfortunately in the service of the Grey Knight. I was forced to yield to him a little less than a month ago. I am no favorite of his and have been poorly treated since I have been with him. However, my honor as a knight keeps me in his service, and he has sent me on this quest to you. Honestly, I think he did it to get rid of me and to put me in the middle of a quarrel."

"How can I know you are not close in his service and sent here to meddle?

"Lord, I can assure you that he sent me here to meddle. I can only guess the purpose, but I am an honorable knight. Would I have helped your son if I wasn't?"

Lord Aelle's body language seemed to concede the point, which encouraged Justus to continue.

"I was sent here on an errand to reclaim a golden cup that the Grey Knight claims to be his. He said I would know this cup by a silver cross with rubies at each point."

Anger settled in Lord Aelle's eyes, "I know the cup."

"I am not to return without it. As I'm sure you can see, lord, the predicament in which this puts me shows what sort of feelings my lord has for me. A cup of such value would not be easily given, especially to one who appears to be your enemy. If it isn't freely given, then I could only resort to things that my honor as a knight would not allow me to do.

"The Grey Knight knew that I was not likely to succeed, and he barred my return if I failed, knowing that my honor would keep me on the quest until I succeeded or died in its pursuit."

"I see that you are in no enviable position," his expression softening toward Justus. "I see my old friend," his voice thick with sarcasm, "is at a game. We too can join him."

Almost before he finished his sentence, the doors to his hall swung open, and a dozen men-at-arms ushered in three bound knights.

"My lord," said one of the sentries, "we came upon these knights sleeping near the first watch. Their violence upon discovery and refusal to name themselves have brought them here to you."

Lord Aelle's wrinkled and tanned face seemed to draw strength from the audacity of the intruders, "From whence have you come? And for what purpose have you dishonored me with the treatment of my men? Answer quickly or perforce you shall compel mine hand." The men remained silent, although fear was plain on their face.

"I know these knights, lord," Justus began, "they are fellow knights under the service of the Grey Knight."

"What have you to say for yourselves?" bellowed Lord Aelle.

The knights looked nervously at one another in silence, none of them willing to be the first to speak.

"Remove them from mine presence and lock them up until I have determined my pleasure." Lord Aelle's men nodded and led the intruders away in silence.

It was several minutes before Lord Aelle broke the silence, "I think I see the mind of the Grey Knight, and I like it not. Should we hear no other news of another body of his knights, we may assume these lackeys meant no direct harm to my person or my holdings, at least not yet. Three knights could accomplish little more than follow Sir Justus, gather information, or act as an emissary from their lord, which they clearly are not, as none of them were inclined to speak. We shall see if time and some little persuasion will part their lips."

13

The Challenge

As it was getting late, Lord Aelle dismissed his son to find quarters for Sir Justus for the evening while he considered the best course of action.

Justus spent the night peacefully in Sir Lorne's household but was delayed in getting to sleep, as word spread quickly of his coming to Sir Lorne's aid. Several retellings were required before Justus finally drifted off to sleep, grateful to be out of the clutches of the Grey Knight, at least for a time.

The next morning, Sir Lorne escorted Justus back to the Great Hall at Lord Aelle's beckoning, "Much thought have I given to these three knights in my keeping. Guile is at play here, and we must meet it in similar fashion. We may yet outwit our opponent at his own game. I deem it best to give these knights seven days to consider their situation. Orders have been given to separate them during this time. At the conclusion of these days, we shall see what we shall see."

Over the course of the following days, Justus spent much of his time with Sir Lorne. The two knights had discovered much in common, and Sir Lorne did not want to waste any opportunity to show his gratitude to his rescuer. Justus received more than his share of attention during this time, his name spreading through the surrounding area, as word of his exploits were told and retold among the people who swore fealty to Lord Aelle. Despite this attention, these few days passed pleasantly for Justus, and he found many companions amongst these good people.

Justus was pleased to hear that, regardless of the dishonorable behavior the three knights displayed on the night of their capture, Lord Aelle displayed his honor by caring well for his prisoners. They stayed comfortably under house arrest with a servant assigned to care for each of their needs. They were well fed, well housed, and were perfectly at their leisure within their confines; however, the knights had no contact with each other. They had no contact with Lord Aelle, either, until the end of the seven days.

On the last day, Lord Aelle and several of his most trusted knights went into the chambers of each of the knights, confronting them on their behavior.

"How come you to lurk about mine stronghold?" Lord Aelle questioned the first knight.

The knight had grown at ease over the past week, given the special care he had received, so he was somewhat taken aback at the menacing group of men that now stood before him.

"Speak! if you value your life," Lord Aelle responded to the silence of the prisoner.

"Your honor would not allow you to slay a knight for silence," the knight nervously growled, hoping Lord Aelle was a better knight than he.

"How speak you of honor?!" raged Lord Aelle. "'Tis always the blackguard looking for mercy who is not willing to grant it himself." He paced the small room for a moment before continuing in a calmer tone, "But 'tis true that I may not slay you for your silence, but you did render violence to my men when you were captured upon mine lands. And impudent silence is all you have rendered me.

"However, similar ends can be gained without murder if you do not wish to reclaim your honor by disclosing your mission in good faith." Lord Aelle's vague threat only increased the nervousness of this knight, who shifted uneasily in his seat.

"Two choices lie before you. You can disclose your purpose, or you can remain silent. If neither you nor your companions speak, be you warned, that you will be fighting in mortal combat with your two other companions.

Battle will continue until only one remains alive. This one will have the honor of delivering a message to the Grey Knight. Anyone who speaks freely before it comes to this will be allowed to return to their lord to deliver a message, being granted their lives with only your shame returning with you – but only if I am satisfied with the answer. If any person speaks out, he will return freely, with those remaining silent flogged before being returned to their lord."

The knight's confusion and fear increased as he sat in silence. His resolution was wavering, and his courage quickly waned without the presence of his two companions. He sensed that Lord Aelle and his men were growing impatient and that time was running out for his decision. If his companions were given the same terms he was, the last thing he wanted was to remain silent while the others spoke, getting flogged to no purpose. He wavered for a moment more before he made up his mind.

"We were sent to follow him, lord," he muttered in a soft voice.

"Sent to follow whom, and speak up!"

"Sir Justus, lord. We were sent to follow Sir Justus." A look of resignation had settled across his face, and all his resolve toppled in the face of his inquisitors.

"Why were you sent thus?"

"My lord has no love for Sir Justus, and he did devise a plan for his undoing. The Grey Knight sent him forth on a quest that would likely bring your wrath upon his head. In the rare chance of Sir Justus completing the quest…," the knight looked around shamefacedly at those in the room before he continued, "and if he achieved success, I was to…we were to fall upon him as he returned. This quest was to be the end of Sir Justus." The knight hung his head and said no more. No more was said to him either, as Sir Aelle led his men out of the room, leaving the knight to his own shame.

Lord Aelle displayed his wisdom and chivalrous bearing with his treatment of the other two knights. He questioned them both in the same manner. For wisdom's sake, he wanted to ensure that their stories coincided. For chivalry's sake, he wanted to ensure that no single knight was to blame and bear the brunt of the punishment. They could not turn on the first knight he questioned and would likely receive a less harsh punishment from their lord.

After the questioning was complete, Lord Aelle met with Sir Lorne and Justus to share what he had learned and to formulate a plan. All three knights had given the same basic story, which Lord Aelle was then inclined to believe. Justus was informed of the Grey Knight's treachery toward him and that Lord Aelle would not abandon him to his plight.

"You have proven yourself a worthy and worshipful knight, and I cannot stand by when such perfidy is to be meted out upon one who came to the aid of my son. We shall soon see how this false lord likes the end of his own game."

"What would you do, lord?" Justus inquired.

"We shall give him what he desires, although methinks that this cup will leave a foul taste in his mouth."

"You mean to give him the cup?" Sir Lorne asked with surprise.

"That is my intent," Lord Aelle replied with a sly grin, "although not in the manner the Grey Knight desires. I say we shall provide a force of 100 knights and men-at-arms to escort these three imprisoned knights and Sir Justus back to the Grey Knight, along with the disputed cup. We can catch this treacherous lord unawares…" Here he paused looking somewhat abashed toward Justus, as his plan hinged on something he had not previously discussed with him. He continued momentarily in a meek tone, "Sir Justus, it appears that in my haste, I did assign a role to you that might require much risk. Pray, hear me out and I will defer to your will."

"Please continue, lord," Justus replied.

"We will catch him unawares, and we will make him earn yon cup that he seeks. If he would take your life, he must do it himself, yet you may get satisfaction for his ill-devised treachery. You shall challenge him to seek justice for his evil. He dare not refuse, if not for pride's sake, then because he will be in no position, as I will demand justice for his attempted theft if he refuses.

"I shall bring the cup with us, thus releasing you from your quest, as you did what was required of you. If he does defeat you, the cup will be given him in exchange for your life. If you defeat him, then it will be his downfall. He will either yield to you and swear fealty, or he will meet his death. No matter which, his lordship over you will be finished. What say you, Sir Justus?"

Justus considered the proposal for a moment before giving his consent, "I will do it."

"Are you sure this is acceptable?" asked Sir Lorne out of concern for the risks to Justus.

The resolution in Justus' voice answered Sir Lorne's concern as well as his words did, "I see no other way - for my honor, for your honor, Lord Aelle, and for justice." He paused a moment before continuing, as if deciding if he should let these men in on a secret. "And because I can no longer be bound to him as my lord. I have lost too much time already."

"Time?" queried Lord Aelle, "What mean you by this?"

Justus recounted the story of his plight, from his fealty to Lord Alden, to the murder and betrayal by Sir Logan, the aid he received from Sientio, and finally his yielding to the Grey Knight. The concern for King Geraint and his inability to accomplish anything for his king was a theme woven throughout his narrative.

"It pains me to hear of Lord Alden's death. He was a goodly knight and a fair lord. No doubt do I have of Prince Broga's hand in this deed. I do like our plan all the more in light of your tale. Much work is there to accomplish, and unseating the Grey Knight must needs be our first step."

"The Grey Knight is not well liked by most of his knights and warriors, so I think there will be many who will join us, although there are a few who we need to keep our eyes on," Justus concluded.

* * *

The next day was spent in preparation for the journey to the Grey Knight's stronghold. Supplies were gathered, orders were given, and weapons were prepared. The bustling community buzzed with excitement as knights and men-at-arms were summoned and women prepared their men for the journey. Lord Aelle assigned a core of trusted warriors to stay with the settlement and defend it at need, but he decided to take the majority of his forces with him.

One hundred warriors and knights rode out the next day, not counting Lord Aelle, Justus, and the three captured knights. The journey back to the Grey Knight was much faster than the journey out, as Lord Aelle knew exactly where to lead his men. In fact, it was early evening the following day when the party approached the desired stronghold.

Riding at the front of his men, Lord Aelle raised a hand, bringing his men to a halt. "Sir Justus and I will ride with ten knights and the rest will follow at a distance of one hundred paces. Once we have secured the gate, the rest will follow us in to the challenge."

A pre-assigned group of knights then rode forward to join Sir Justus and Lord Aelle, and they rode ahead to the stronghold. The rest of the men did not resume their course until the agreed upon distance between the two groups had been reached.

Sir Justus announced his approach to the sentries at the gate, "I have completed my quest and have returned."

The sentries on duty were among the majority of the Grey Knight's warriors, in that they both liked and respected Sir Justus. They also were not of the few who were privy to their lord's plot against him. Thus, they felt completely justified letting the small group through the gates.

As soon as Justus and his companions passed through the gates, the rest of Lord Aelle's men descended upon the unsuspecting sentries and relieved them of their duties. The stealth of Lord Aelle's plans and the speed with which his men entered the Grey Knight's stronghold ensured that there was virtually no resistance.

The large group of men approaching their lord's great hall caused the men-at-arms guarding its door to snap to attention. Despite their confusion, they wanted to make a good show of themselves in front of the oncoming mass of men. As Lord Aelle, Sir Justus, ten knights, and the three prisoners approached them, they questioned the business of the intruders.

Sir Justus replied, "Warriors, I have returned from the quest our lord sent me on. Please announce my return."

The strange lord and his large group of men made the men-at-arms nervous, but they were glad to see Sir Justus' safe return. A sentry disappeared inside the hall to announce Sir Justus. He soon returned with an anxious look on his face.

"Sir Justus, I have been instructed that you alone are to enter the hall."

Lord Aelle stepped in before Justus could reply, "Good men, you are relieved of your duties this night." As he said this, he motioned for some of his men to escort the warriors away. Once removed, the small group moved inside the hall.

Sir Justus was the first to address the Grey Knight, "I have returned, my lord. I was successful on my quest and have returned with the cup. However, these three knights of yours were somewhat less successful."

The three bound knights were presented to their lord. His face hardened, and anger flashed in his eyes. A steely glance was briefly cast on Sir Camlin, whose face was covered with a look of genuine surprise. However, he quickly mastered himself, and anger mixed with hatred soon dominated his countenance.

"To what do I owe the pleasure of your company?" the Grey Knight addressed Lord Aelle with venom in his voice.

"I come bearing the cup you covet. Was this not the purpose of Sir Justus' quest?" Lord Aelle replied calmly. "However, 'twill be no easy task for this cup to remain in your possession."

Justus continued, "Lord, you sent me on a quest designed for my harm, and you dishonored three of your knights in sending them after me. You have also dishonored yourself as a lord and knight. I demand justice."

"You have no right…," the Grey Knight began before he was cut off by Lord Aelle's booming voice.

"Silence, rogue! You will hear him out in full." He motioned for his men to control the room.

His knights quickly drew swords and spread throughout the hall, disarming the few unprepared warriors in the room. Once Lord Aelle's dominance was established, Justus continued.

"I demand justice for your dishonor and your plot against my life. I come to issue you a challenge. If you defeat me, you can have the cup you sent me to retrieve. If I best you, then you are undone."

"What if I do not accept this challenge?" contempt thick in the Grey Knight's reply.

"You will accept," Lord Aelle put in threateningly. "The laws of chivalry demand it, and I and my men will ensure this rightful challenge. 'Tis your only choice, as you are not equipped to repulse me. Ninety more knights and warriors will ensure that."

Impotent fury rose within the Grey Knight as he began to understand his situation. He had no choice but to accept the challenge, and he and his men were brought from his hall and out to a flat, open area that was being prepared for the fight by Lord Aelle's men.

As the word of the challenge spread throughout the community, people of all ages and ranks appeared for the spectacle. Justus and the Grey Knight were each being prepared by their respective supporters for the fight. Justus had been outfitted by Lord Aelle, to replace the poor weaponry that his lord had given him for the quest.

As the time quickly approached to commence, and the assembled crowd had fallen into place, Justus looked about him, scanning his environment to distract him from his nerves. After completing the examination of his surroundings, he felt the vague impression that something was not as it should be, although he could not place his finger on it. He quickly scrutinized the crowd again, sharpening the vague impression into a strong feeling that something was missing, or someone.

He racked his brain for the few remaining moments before he and the Grey Knight assumed their positions, but without success. Finally, as he faced his opponent, seeing only the Grey Knight's hate-filled eyes through his helmet visor, it struck him.

"Sir Camlin!" Justus shouted. "Where is Sir Camlin?!"

He looked about him, and a commotion in the crowd gained him attention. He saw Sir Camlin rushing at Lord Aelle, intent on death.

"Lord Aelle!" Justus yelled. "Look out behind you; defend yourself!"

As the crowd's attention was pulled to where Sir Justus was pointing, an angry yell came from Justus' left, and he realized that the Grey Knight had taken advantage of his momentary distraction. Justus barely had time to turn toward his attacker and raise his shield. The blow he received knocked him back, but he was able to quickly regain his balance and was better prepared for the second blow that quickly followed. Justus deftly deflected the blow, fixing his complete focus on his opponent.

From his previous battle with the Grey Knight, Justus knew the power and endurance of his enemy. But he also knew that he could be sloppy. Justus' focus intensified, and everything in his environment slowly faded from view. His opponent seemed to be the only thing that existed for him, and time seemed to tick off more slowly than before. Justus took in every move his opponent made, and the opportunity to attack soon presented itself.

The Grey Knight hefted his sword in the air and made to deal a killing blow, hoping to take advantage of his surprise attack. The downward stroke was crushing and swift. It sliced through the air and into the dirt at his feet. Justus had deftly spun away, causing the blow to miss. The gargantuan effort behind the blow and the unexpected miss left his opponent off-balance. Justus quickly closed the few paces between himself and the Grey Knight. He slammed his shield into his foe's, putting the whole force of his body behind the blow.

Falling backward, the Grey Knight stepped on the flat of his sword, pulling the hilt from his hand. He tripped over his feet and fell on his back. He quickly rolled and rose to one knee before Justus was on him. Justus rained several hard blows in rapid succession onto his adversary's shield, driving him down to his back again. Justus slammed one more ferocious blow on the shield, cracking it from top to bottom, shivering the Grey Knight's arm, which dropped uselessly to his side. Justus stood above him with his sword at his enemy's neck. "Remove your helmet," Justus growled through gritted teeth.

The Grey Knight slowly doffed his helmet, struggling through the pain in his shield arm. A mixture of malicious anger and shame darkened his eyes, knowing his defeat was at hand.

Then Justus spoke the words he dreaded most, "Do you yield?"

"I would sooner die than yield to you," he replied, the hate thick in his words.

Without taking his eyes off his opponent, Justus called out to the crowd, "You have all heard his refusal to yield. By rights, his life is mine and all that he has called his own. However, I choose to grant mercy where none would have been shown to me. Men at arms, strip him of his armor and guard him well."

Five of Lord Aelle's household soldiers came forward and led the Grey Knight away in defeat. Justus scanned the crowd for Lord Aelle and found him whole and hale with the assassin, Sir Camlin, dead at his feet. The attempt had failed, and the rogue lord had been unseated.

Justus called out to the crowd again, "The Grey Knight's lordship has been broken. Your fealty to him is no more. Any who swear fealty to me will be welcomed. I will give you tonight to make your decision." With that, the crowd began to slowly disperse, and Justus rejoined Lord Aelle and his men.

"We have much to discuss this night," said Lord Aelle, as he congratulated Justus with a clap on the back.

14

The Landless Lord

The men at arms set up camp for the night and posted watch, while Lord Aelle, his knights, and Justus moved into the great hall. The men ate much and toasted much in celebration of Sir Justus' victory over the Grey Knight. However, Lord Aelle and Justus remained sober in the face of the decisions in front of them. As the celebration died down, and the men made their way off to bed, Lord Aelle, Sir Lorne, and Justus sat by the fire in the hearth to determine their next steps.

"Tomorrow will see you proclaimed lord of these lands," Lord Aelle began. "For that I congratulate you."

"No lord, I can't be lord of these lands."

Sir Lorne joined in supporting his father's claim, "These lands are yours by right. You have defeated their lord."

"Lord Aelle, I give them to you."

Lord Aelle started to rise from his seat in surprise. He paused a moment before sitting back down, "'Tis a wondrous gift to bestow, but in no wise can I accept this lordship as a gift."

"Lord, it is not a gift I give lightly, but you need to understand me. I will accept lordship, but I will not accept the land." Seeing the confusion on his companions' faces, he continued. "I don't have the time to care for people and lands and disputes and crops and all else that comes with being a lord.

There is a threat to our king and our way of life in the person of Prince Broga. I mean to do nothing but work toward defeating him. The only way that I myself can raise an army is to be a lord, but I can't be encumbered with the responsibility of the land. So, I give it to you."

"A landless lord…," Lord Aelle mused, mulling over the foreign concept in his mind. A few moments passed before making his reply. "Such a thing has not been done and should not be done. A lord without lands is as a sword with no arm to wield it. Therefore, I propose you a temporary agreement. I will take these lands of yours and be steward of them. Should you succeed in this quest, you may return and make claim to them. In the meantime, you will be steward of mine forces and use them to accomplish your purposes."

"Agreed," replied Justus, hope finally returning to his heart.

"Well then," spoke Lord Aelle as he stood. "To bed with us, and tomorrow will bring what it will."

All three men left the hearth and found a place in the hall to sleep. Justus found some animal skins that had been left for him and made a bed for himself near the fire. He lay watching the orange flames licking up the dry wood. The crackling and popping of the fire created a pleasant melody that helped melt away the tension, and Justus fell asleep.

* * *

The morning sun shone brightly on the stronghold, as if in celebration of yesterday's events. Justus rose shortly after the sun did and was met by Lord Aelle as they broke their fast in the great hall.

"What do you think we'll find out there today?" Justus asked with a nervous edge to his voice.

"We soon shall see," Lord Aelle replied. "No matter what we find, it will be better than what we faced when the sun arose yesterday morn."

Justus nodded his head in agreement and rose to discover what fate would bring him. He stepped outside the great hall with Lord Aelle behind and was greeted by a multitude of shouts and cheers. Hundreds of people had gathered together to proclaim their support for the victor.

Lord Aelle stepped forward and loudly announced what the crowd already knew, "Sir Justus you are no more. I proclaim you Lord Justus, victor over the Grey Knight and ruler of all that he did possess."

The crowd erupted in cheers at the proclamation. After a few moments, he silenced them with his hand. "I want to say in front of everyone here that my lordship will be unlike any that you've seen. It has to be. The Black Prince moves upon the land, and I fear for our king. I have vowed to use all of my strength to see the threat gone and our king safe. I have spoken with Lord Aelle, and he has agreed to stewardship over my holdings until my quest is over. In turn, he has granted me stewardship over his men to use as needed to rid ourselves of Prince Broga's threat.

"I invite any of you who were under the Grey Knight's lordship to swear fealty to me; you are also free to go if you so choose. Now is the moment of choice."

Men streamed from the crowd to lay their weapons at Lord Justus' feet and pledge their fealty to him. Only a small handful had departed during the night, leaving much of the Grey Knight's battle host intact. Justus found the men all too willing to shed the shackles of their former lord and embrace the leadership of one whom they had grown to respect. Many had continued their martial practices in Justus' absence, further honing their skills. The men were better warriors because of Justus' leadership and initiative, and they were glad to pledge themselves to him.

After all the remaining men pledged their allegiances to their new Lord, the crowd was dismissed to their work and to their homes, and Justus met with Lord Aelle, Sir Lorne, and other trusted men to determine their course of action.

"Lord Aelle, what do you suggest?" asked Justus once they had gained the hall. Lord Aelle nodded his head slightly, acknowledging the new lord's deference to his experience.

"Prince Broga must be dealt with, but no body of men have we that can do this now. We must needs muster loyal forces. There are those loyal to the king that will aid our endeavor."

"We should send messengers, then – tomorrow," replied Justus.

"Yes," confirmed Lord Aelle, "we must wait no longer. Choose those that are trustworthy and ride well, for speed is of great import."

"Father, I would have you send me," Sir Lorne joined in. Several others present also volunteered.

"Yes, my son. You are a goodly rider, and none do I trust more. I charge you to choose amongst my men and administer my will in this."

"That I will, father," a proud smile played across Sir Lorne's face.

"How long do we wait for news of our allies?" asked Justus. "How much time do we give them before we act?" The need to begin was palpable in Justus' voice.

"Two weeks and no longer, we must act soon. Our king may be in need even now. We will have them rally here in a fortnight and assess our strength at that time."

Food and drink was called to the board as the men discussed their plans into the evening. Loyal lords were named and messenger assignments were given. The men would ride out at dawn and were to return word within a fortnight of the support from the loyal lords. After orders were dispensed and bellies filled, the evening drew to a close, and the men dispersed to sleep.

Justus, however, was not so fortunate in finding sleep. He lie awake in his new hall, wondering at his fortunes. Never did he imagine himself a lord, a man of influence and power. He called up bittersweet memories of his tutelage under Sir Logan and his fealty to Lord Alden. The hunt where he saved Sir Bana's life seemed like ages ago. He thought of the betrayal of his lord with deep sadness and his subsequent aimless wandering. He uttered a silent prayer of thanks for the saving presence of Sientio and for his deliverance during his several martial encounters. He prayed for the safety of the king and for success in tomorrow's mission. He prayed for wisdom and guidance as a lord and in his quest against the evil Prince Broga. Justus continued to pray fervently into the night until sleep finally captured him.

* * *

Dawn broke with low clouds and a misty drizzle. Justus was up soon after the sun, and he gathered his messengers for final instructions, Lord Aelle doing the same. When all was said that was needed, Justus called out a final word of encouragement, "May God grant you speed and success. Fly to us with word as soon as you can."

Lord Aelle then added his encouragement, "Godspeed men. These are ill-fated times, and you do play a role crucial to the safety of your king. God's blessings be upon you."

With that, the messengers departed on their steeds with all speed, hoping to find lords to aid their cause. Justus and Lord Aelle stood watching them until they rode out of sight, silently willing their quest to success.

"Now we wait," concluded Justus sullenly when the riders were no longer in view.

"We wait, yes, but we shall prepare. There is much to do in the next fortnight," replied Lord Aelle, hoping to encourage Justus into action.

"Yes, much to do," Justus shook his head slightly, as if wresting himself from a reverie and turned toward Lord Aelle, his eyes now sharp and focused, "and not much time."

Lord Aelle withdrew to prepare his men, and Justus did the same. Orders were given, and the stronghold hummed with activity. Men were sharpening weapons and building food stores, blacksmiths repaired damaged weapons and armor, as well as adding to the supply of new weapons. Women repaired clothes and made new ones, as well as baking bread and salting meat. Young warriors continued their training, hoping to add to their rudimentary skills. Experienced warriors trained to keep sharp. Not a soul in the encampment was idle, morning to night, with preparations. This went on for several days before the first of the messengers returned.

Justus and Lord Aelle were alerted when the first messenger arrived and rushed to greet him. "What news?" questioned Lord Aelle, eager to begin receiving word.

"I am sorry lord. Lord Earh sends his regrets. He claims he has no men to spare, as the Black Prince is harrying his lands. Give up his men he will not."

"Prince Broga will continue to harry his lands if we don't defeat him. Doesn't he understand this?" Justus exclaimed in exasperation.

"Patience, Lord Justus," Lord Aelle said calmly, "we shall see what other messengers bring."

Two more messengers arrived that day with similar refusals, causing Justus to become very concerned. He and Lord Aelle could field three hundred men against the Black Prince, but he knew that he would need much greater numbers to overcome this enemy.

Four more messengers arrived the next day, all with refusals. Seven messengers out of twenty had returned and none had brought news of help. The following day, the sixth since the riders had departed, saw ten of them return. The first ray of hope arrived with these riders, as five of them reported the lords they had visited would be arriving in force on the arranged date.

Despite the good news of help, Justus' hope was faltering. Of the seventeen messengers who had returned, only five were successful in bringing a word of good news. The reign of terror that Prince Broga was wreaking on the land must be worse than he had imagined. Justus also wondered at the mass of forces at the Black Prince's command to cow so many 'loyal' lords into submission. Justus fell asleep that night with another prayer on his lips for good news to arrive tomorrow.

In this, he was not disappointed. Despite the news of refusals from the first two riders who returned that day, the final messenger returned, buoyed by the hope of his good news. Encouraged by his bearing, Justus and Lord Aelle came to greet him.

"Happy news, good lords," he said breathlessly as he entered the stronghold. Justus and Lord Aelle waited impatiently while he caught his breath. "I have ridden from the hall of the noble Lord Conall. He has been mustering a battle force these past weeks to face the Black Prince, and he is wonderly glad to hear of allies. In two days, he will begin his march here with well-nigh one thousand men, warriors and knights all."

"'Tis blessed news. Lord Conall is a foe not to be taken lightly, and 'tis a boon to our quest."

"Yes, this is wonderful news," Justus added cheerfully. "This may be just what we needed."

Evening was wearing on when this last messenger had arrived, so Justus invited all the messengers to the hall to sup at the board with him and Lord Aelle. After they ate and drank their fill, each of them was given another assignment. They were to ride the land in pairs and search out the position and strength of Prince Broga and return within seven days. They were promptly dismissed to a good night's sleep, while Lord Aelle and Justus took stock of their situation.

"We shall soon see how it lies," commented Lord Aelle without enthusiasm.

"Yes, I had expected more, too," replied Justus, knowing the reason for his friend's discouragement. "Six lords out of twenty is not much, but those who are with us are good, loyal lords."

"It is as you say," Lord Aelle replied blandly.

"You and I supply three hundred men. Lord Conall will supply one thousand. We can figure another thousand from the five remaining lords. That is quite a battle host."

"I fear the treachery of the Black Prince runs deep and that our forces will be vastly outnumbered," Lord Aelle countered, revealing the source of his gloom.

"Lord, we are fighting for our king, our lands, our life. Prince Broga is fighting for greed. Loyalty and bravery is a powerful force multiplier."

"I doubt not the resolve of our men…"

Justus cut him off quickly, "then doubt not your own resolve. Your confidence needs to be greater than that of your men if we hope to succeed."

"It is good to hear your confidence," he said.

"Lord Aelle, we can't be anything less than confident. We will win this war against the Black Prince and restore the king to his throne, should he still be alive."

"How can you know?"

"Because we have to." The calm confidence with which Justus spoke seemed enough for Lord Aelle.

He nodded his head, grim resolve on his face, "Without victory, there is nothing else for us. Win we must." He stood and left the hall. His walk was strong and purposeful as he went to his quarters for the night. Justus also prepared for sleep and was soon in slumber's embrace, resting in the peace that hope provided.

* * *

The next day, Justus began to get impatient, as he was tired of the waiting and was ready for action. He decided to saddle his horse and ride around and see the lands he had just granted into the care of Lord Aelle. Justus located Sir Lorne and asked him to accompany him on his ride.

"'Twould be a welcome diversion. Waiting is a skill that practice does not make less odious. I would be glad to ride with you."

Justus saddled Bayard, who he had found shortly after his victory over the Grey Knight, and armed himself with a sword. Sir Lorne arrayed himself similarly, and they set off, passing out of the stronghold gates at a canter. They spent the morning riding and were able to put a fair distance between themselves and the stronghold. They had left his new lands more than half an hour previously, and they continued to ride, exploring the area outside of their holdings when they saw riders on a hilltop clearing in the distance.

"Let's follow them and see who they are," said Justus, excited with the possibility of purposeful action.

"I agree, lord, but we must take all caution not to be discovered until we can be sure if yon riders are friend or foe."

"True. We must be careful not to be seen."

Justus and Sir Lorne spurred their horses to speed in an attempt to close the distance between them and the unknown riders. As they rode, they watched the riders disappear into a wood, and they turned their horses toward the strangers projected path. They rode for twenty minutes more before slowing down and taking care to not make excess noise.

Fortunately, the riders they sought were not taking the same care. Justus and Sir Lorne heard the riders before they saw them, hearing voices speaking through a stand of trees. They dismounted and tethered their horses to a tree, so as to ensure more quiet progress toward the voices. As they moved silently closer, the voices resolved themselves into clarity.

"I ha'n't seen no men 'round these parts yet," sounded one voice.

"I assure you that they must needs be not too far afield. The Grey Knight did say that we should be coming near," replied a companion.

Justus and Sir Lorne were both surprised when a honey-tongued feminine voice replied confidently, "We will find them. We come not to enjoin them, as you know well. Just close enough so that I may see the stronghold and lay such curses as I can upon them."

A chill ran up Justus' spine as he heard the malice in the voice. He and Sir Lorne crept silently under the cover of the undergrowth until they had the enemy party in their site. Half a dozen knights had dismounted and were watering their horses at a small stream. The knights were arrayed in dull black armor with the image of a dragon etched in each of their shields. The woman who accompanied them was still seated on her horse. Her bearing was regal and proud. She wore a fine, silken black shirt underneath a black, hardened leather breastplate, upon which a dragon was emblazoned in red. A skirt of sturdy, black material flowed out from underneath the breastplate. A sword at her side caught Justus' eye. What was not encased in the scabbard looked exquisite, having a hilt of intertwined silver and gold with a large emerald on the pommel, brilliantly reflecting the sunlight. She removed her helmet to allow her head to breathe on their short rest, releasing a mane of glossy, jet black hair that fell down her back. She shook her head to allow her hair to freely cascade down.

Sir Lorne spoke of the woman first, "'Tis the witch, the accursed wife of the Black Prince," he breathed in disgust.

Seeing the woman's face made Justus fall back in shock. The only words he could utter were, "Lady Draic!"

15

On Death's Door

"Sir, it's nigh upon noon, and I thought it prudent to awaken you." The fog of sleep lay heavy on Justus, as he heard a voice above him and felt someone gently shaking his shoulder. "Sir, it may be best for you to rouse yourself for the day."

"Is that you, Clive?" was all Justus could muster for the moment.

"It is," replied the butler. "The day approaches noon, and I believed it best to awaken you, if for no other reason than to give you an update on your wife's condition."

That quickly brought Justus to attention, "Anna, yes, how is she?" he said, sitting up quickly.

"Not good, I'm afraid, sir. She appears to be on death's door. I fear we may only have one or two more nights before she is lost. You may want to go to the hospital before the day is too far gone."

Justus hung his head, grieving for his young wife, whose life was ebbing away.

"Sir, this may not be the time, but I was wondering if you dreamt anything last night that might be useful to us."

Justus snapped his head back up, the fire rekindling in his eyes. "Yes, I did dream last night. I'll tell you Clive, I've never experienced anything like it. The dreams are so *real* and can seem to last for months at a time. When I'm in them, I forget that it isn't reality." He paused for a moment, as if in the act of remembering something important. "And *she* was there. It was her, the woman in the sarcophagus. I saw her with my own eyes. In fact, she was even carrying the sword that we saw with her on her horse. I'm sure it was her. Clive, I don't know that this tells us exactly what we need to do, but it seems clear that this has something to do with that woman."

"Do you have any idea who the woman is?"

"Yes, I do actually. Her name is Lady Draic. She is the wife of a murderous and usurping prince in my dreams. Some believe her to be some sort of witch, who drives the evil schemes of her husband. I saw her for the first time right before you woke me up, and she was up to no good.

"Well Clive, I've got a lot to think about, and I want to be by Anna's side as much as I can today. I want you to think about the situation as well, and see if you can come up with some ideas."

"I will, sir, and I will be praying."

"Thank you Clive, we need all the prayers we can get."

With that, Justus headed for the hospital and was saddened by his wife's condition when he arrived at her bedside. Her breaths were still regular, but Justus thought them much too shallow. She seemed to sleep most of the time, but this was interrupted by occasional delirious mumblings, accompanied by some weak, agitated movements. Justus tried to catch the words she was saying, but she was too weak to speak loudly, and it seemed like nothing but gibberish to him.

He spent the long, arduous day at her bedside. Although sitting in silence with her the whole day, fighting off the grief and impatience physically exhausted him. Finally, the sun started its descent, and he decided that it was time for him to go. He gently kissed Anna on the forehead, said a quick prayer for her and for him, and he left the room to head back home.

Clive met him at the door when he arrived, "How is she doing, sir?"

"No major changes, Clive. It's so hard to see her like this. She was strong and vibrant, and now she's bed ridden and almost too weak to move. I'm afraid that tonight is my last chance to find out any more useful information. I think she's too weak to last much longer."

"Let us talk further inside. I have the table set for you, and hot food may ease your mind, if even for a moment."

"Thank you Clive. You've been a big help through all of this."

Justus followed Clive to the kitchen where they ate a supper of Cornish game hen, roasted red potatoes, and thickly sliced bread. Despite having all day to ponder their predicament, neither of them had gotten any closer to solving the mystery, and they spent the dinner commiserating with each other about their helplessness.

After supper was over, Clive set about cleaning up the kitchen, as Justus remained at the table in contemplative silence. Even after Clive had finished his work, Justus remained as he was.

Clive sat down opposite Justus and stirred him from his troubled thoughts, "Sir, if I may be so bold, might I suggest that you retire to the library. The evening is drawing on, and it may be that the earlier you begin your reading, the more time you have to discover what you might do."

"You're right Clive. It doesn't do anyone any good me sulking here in the kitchen." Looking at his watch, he continued, "It's after nine o'clock anyway. Don't let me sleep in 'til noon tomorrow. I'd like to spend the day with Anna." He stood up and left the kitchen sullenly. Heading into the library, he shut the door behind him, located the book, and settled down to read.

* * *

Justus and Sir Lorne were tearing through the woods on horseback, heading back to the security of their stronghold. It wasn't until they had shut the gates behind them and summoned Lord Aelle and other war leaders before they began their discourse.

"They are at our very doorsteps!" shouted Sir Lorne, pounding his fist on the table for emphasis.

"What is this that you speak of?" demanded Lord Aelle.

"Prince Broga has sent his witch of a wife and a small party to search us out, and we did espy them in the very act."

"There were six knights with her," added Justus. "We heard them say they were looking for our location, and we rode away as fast as we could. I don't think they knew we were there," he said in anticipation of the obvious next question.

"Verily, this does change things," Lord Aelle responded, the concern obvious in his voice. "Alas, there is naught to be done until the lords who pledged us aid have arrived. I shall double the sentries and pray that battle is not brought to us too soon. We are now but two days until the pledged lords are to join us in their full strength. Let us hope they have not been delayed."

In that, Lord Aelle was not disappointed, as the first of the allied lords arrived the following day, as well as the scouting parties to announce the location of Prince Broga's army. The advance scouts quickly informed the lords Aelle and Justus that the main encampment of Prince Broga was but a day's march from their location. This was of obvious concern, but the scouts quickly allayed their fears.

"My lords, there is no indication that the rogue prince seeks you out to engage in a martial encounter. It does seem that he is content to wait for you at present."

"Praise the Good God for this, at least," replied Lord Aelle with some relief. "Methinks that the prince puts much store in his confidence. How many men do you think have thrown in their lot with the Black Prince?"

To this the scout replied with some reluctance, "My lords, I fear that he has gathered well nigh to ten thousand warriors."

"Ten thousand…," Justus echoed in despair. "We reckoned less than twenty-five hundred for ourselves. How are we supposed to take on four times our number?"

"Lord Justus," Lord Aelle turned to his friend, "cross not the bridge before you arrive. Much can happen before war is enjoined. Discard not hope before it has been tested."

"You're right," Justus replied. "If I'm going to lead our men, I've got a lot to do before we fight, and that doesn't include worrying about things I can't control."

The meeting with the scouts reminded Justus that he set the example for his men, and they deserved nothing less from him than his best. He was reinvigorated with energy and set to coming up with a plan to undermine the advantage Prince Broga's numbers gave him. He gathered several trusted knights, briefed them on his plan, and waited until the cover of darkness before departing for the enemy camp.

The men rode lightly and quickly through the darkening night, the thick clouds blocking out the celestial lights. The inky blackness did little to slow the riders, however, as they pressed on toward Prince Broga's encampment. As they soon discovered, Prince Broga chose his position well.

He had pitched his tent atop a tor, which afforded a commanding view of the surrounding countryside. His vast army arrayed itself in front and to the sides of the hill. Warriors had not been deployed to the rear, because the terrain made it virtually unassailable. The tor abutted a bend in a river, whose banks had been cut deep over the centuries. It would be impossible to lead an army across the river, up the cliff-like far bank, and scale the tor to overwhelm its defenders. By choosing this location, Prince Broga had determined how his enemy would approach him and where the battle would be fought.

The presence of several of Prince Broga's scouts on the far side of the river did not go unnoticed by Justus and his men, so they tethered their horses in a stand of trees not far from the water and proceeded on foot in the hopes to avoid detection. Caution and the preternatural darkness aided their designs, and they reached the bank of the river unmolested. Holding their weapons above their heads, they forded the river, crossing to the far side and regrouping at the base of the cliff.

Despite the impossibility of leading an army across the water and up the hill, a small group of men could hold out hope of not being detected. This was the aim of Justus and his men. To learn the designs of the enemy on the eve of battle could help turn the tide for the greatly outnumbered loyal forces.

The men replaced their weapons and found sufficient hand and footholds to work their way slowly up the bank. Upon scaling the cliff, the men quickly made their way behind a large boulder, taking cover before deciding their next move.

"My lord," whispered one of the knights next to Justus, "methinks that yon fire does mark Prince Broga's tent. It seems to me that we may yet reach his tent unnoticed."

"Truly, my lord," whispered another voice, "I see not one sentry on the backside of this hill."

"By the Rood," sounded a third, "this night is black, but it aids in our designs. What think you, lord? Shall we proceed?"

"Yes, let's go," was Justus' barely audible reply, "but once we leave this rock we have to keep together; we can't afford to be separated in this darkness."

Justus then crept from behind the boulder and noiselessly made his way up the hill. His companion's assessment was correct; Prince Broga deemed himself safe on the Tor and had placed no sentries behind his tent. This allowed the men to climb the hill without detection, settling in quietly behind the tent. Not hearing any voices inside, Justus sent one of his men to discover what he could and return as quickly as possible.

The knight was not gone long when he returned with news, "Prince Broga and his advisors do sit beside the fire we espied earlier. A brace of large boulders lie not far off and will provide us cover close enough to hear."

"Lead us," was all Justus whispered, as the men quickly followed to their destination. Once settled, the large fire provided ample light to view the proceedings, but the fire struggled to cast its light into the blackness of the night, which provided complete cover for Justus and his men.

"Why does that ungrateful woman tarry?" growled the angry voice of Prince Broga, who was pacing by the fire.

"My lord," soothed Lady Draic, "let not impatience disconcert you on the eve of your great victory. A few moments more, I am sure."

Just then movement on the far side of the fire's circle of light resolved itself into two figures. One was a tall, stout warrior leading a bent old woman into the light. Her wrinkled face and hard, grey eyes were made even uglier by the shadows the firelight cast on her.

"So good of you to come, wise banfaith," said Prince Broga irritably.

A whisper sounded next to Justus' ear, "No banfaith is she. 'Tis a witch and no more."

The old woman bowed her head in nominal obeisance, but remained silent.

"What good word have you for me on this eve of battle?" intoned Prince Broga.

The old woman remained silent for a moment before lifting her gnarled hands toward the sky and making pronouncement, "Beware the landless lord! For he wilt cause thee great troubles. Yet an attempt on thy life thou wilt overcome." With that, the woman dropped her hands and lapsed into silence.

The prophecy seemed to have an immediate effect on Prince Broga. He clearly had not expected a warning and an attempt on his life. He immediately barked out an order to increase the number in his personal body guard. The old woman was led away the same way that she came, and the group around the fire remained silent until she was well away.

"Why does that accursed witch speak thus in riddles?" growled Prince Broga. "I know not what to make of her prattling." He turned to his advisors, "What means she by 'landless lord'? Have you any knowledge of such a person?"

A man stepped forward, his face now well lit by the fire, "My lord, such a thing cannot exist. A lord is made by his lands. This cannot be." Justus recognized him as Lord Scand, the murderous rogue responsible for the death of Lord Alden.

Lady Draic also spoke up, "Be not troubled, husband, for even if your banfaith's words prove true, she has forecast neither defeat nor death for you."

"Yet I will be cautious," he responded forcefully. "I dare not risk overmuch by ignoring her words, mad though she may sound.

"Sir Logan, come hither," called the prince.

A large form moved out of the shadows and into the light. Justus recoiled in shock at the sight of the traitor, his former friend.

"Yes, my lord," Sir Logan replied flatly.

"See to it that only the most trustworthy are placed in my bodyguard and within the hour. You will also ride with me on the morrow to treat with the enemy. So, sleep well; no watch will you endure this night."

Sir Logan bowed his head and dissolved back into the shadows. Prince Broga then dismissed the advisors, and he retired with his wife to his tent.

Justus recovered quickly from the shock of seeing Sir Logan, and he shifted nearer to Broga's tent in an attempt to overhear any additional intelligence.

"I tell you, do not let that old woman have such sway over you." Justus could make out Lady Draic's irritated voice coming from inside the tent.

Prince Broga responded, also with irritation. "Ultimate victory is in our grasp. Why does the ancient hag need to wag her tongue in riddles?"

"I tell you, worry not." Her voice dropped, as if she was about to share a secret. "I have been toiling over something significant, and a breakthrough has been achieved. See this book in my hands?"

"Why show me a book?" he asked dismissively.

"I have discovered a way to tie my life force to this book. Even if I shall die, my body can be brought back to life by the reading of this book, which will drain the life force of the reader, unbeknownst to them. If they keep reading, they will grow weaker and weaker. The same will occur if they stop. My life will return to me as theirs is drained from them. The magic is complicated and imprecise, and I know not else the magic may trigger, but I know my life is preserved in this book forever."

"What does this mean for me, woman? No prophecy was wielded against you."

Sighing in frustration Lady Draic continued, "I needed to recover my strength after this, my first success with this book, but I have another." Justus imagined that the faint rustling in the tent was another book being pulled from amongst her belongings. "This book is for you, and tomorrow night the conditions will be right for the magic to be replicated. After tomorrow night, it will matter not what happens on the field of battle to you, as you can't truly die, as long as this book is safe."

Startled by what he had heard, Justus retreated with his men down the hill, across the river, and back to his own stronghold unseen by the enemy.

He immediately called a council of war with Lord Aelle and his trusted battle chiefs. Justus discussed what was seen and heard, especially with the prophecy. He decided to speak nothing of what Lady Draic said inside the tent, as it seemed far-fetched, and he didn't want to stir the lords up to hasty action.

"The landless lord, eh?" mused Lord Aelle. "Methinks that this witch does caution Prince Broga against you, my lord Justus."

"On the surface, it seems so, and I hope that means good things for us. But what about the attempt on his life? It appears that he will survive, and there was no mention of who would win."

"'Tis true, Lord Justus, but we must accept the will of the Good Lord in these matters, who has entrusted us with the responsibility of doing not less than our utmost. We shall enjoin battle and let come what may."

"Have you made any battle plans?" asked Justus.

"Nay, but we have received summons from Prince Broga to treat with him at noon. Our men have already started to make our encampment not far from the field of battle. I have nominated you to all of the faithful lords to be at the head of our armies. You are 'the landless lord' and best placed to lead. Will you lead us to our fate?"

"You have proffered his name to lead, Lord Aelle, but a decision is yet lacking before asking this of him." The speaker was Lord Edan, a lord loyal to his king, but given to fits of anger and stubbornness. "I know not this newcomer," pointing to Justus. "What proof of valor, what prowess at arms, what loyalty to the king has this lord proved to match mine? Let me lead our armies. Shall I not flay the skin of mine enemy? Shall I not grind the bones of yon faithless army to dust? I say I shall! Death shall come to the Black Prince when next mine eyes light upon the rogue. Let not him think himself safe even at parley!"

"Lord Edan!" shouted Lord Aelle, slamming his open hand on the table. "Douse your fiery tongue. Overstep not the bounds of your honor."

Lord Edan fired back, "What honor shall you cling to in defeat? What honor has the foul prince clung to? Speak not to me of honor when our common enemy has so besmirched it and tossed it aside like a filthy rag."

"As head of this council, I declare that you shall not accompany us to parley on the morrow. I dare not allow you to sully the honor of this council by violating honor's code. The time bound traditions shall be upheld, and safety shall be vouchsafed to our enemies while we meet."

"What say you, fellow lords?" asked Lord Edan. "Do you align yourself with me and behead the snake when least expected or shall you go to your graves with honor and naught else?"

Lord Conall stood to his full height and spoke out in his strong, deep voice, "May you win much honor upon the battlefield, striking the head from the serpent, but you shall have no opportunity to do so on the morrow."

The other lords voiced their assent with Lord Aelle and Lord Conall. Seeing a brick wall of opposition, Lord Edan grew red with anger and stormed out of the council chamber.

Without sitting, Lord Conall turned to Justus, "Lord Justus, Lord Aelle speaks for us all when he did offer you our armies. Will you accept?"

Justus hesitated in the face of such incredible responsibility, but he knew that declining the position would alter little of what they all would have to face tomorrow.

"I will do it," Justus accepted grimly.

"Good," Lord Aelle replied with a solemn nod. Clearly, he was not relishing the prospect of what tomorrow held for everyone in the room and the armies that upheld them. "We ride out at noon to meet the treacherous prince. For my part, I believe a delay shall do us no harm. Avoiding open war on the morrow may give us time to establish a gambit that will advance our interests. In the meantime, let us to bed; we shall need our rest." With that, the men dispersed, mere hours standing between them and their fate.

16

The Final Battle

The short hours of the night sped by too quickly for Justus. He arose to meet the day, dreading what lay before them all. Only too well did he know the incredible odds they faced and how much was at stake. He tried in vain to not dwell on the dire prospects of this day, as he readied himself to meet the enemy at noon. He ate a quick breakfast before equipping Bayard for the fateful ride. Donning his armor and arming himself, he met with Lord Aelle and the rest of the lords and an escort of knights to ride out from their encampment to survey the enemy.

"'Tis but a league that stands between us and the fate God has declared," mused Lord Aelle. "Let us ride forth and see what we may." The men covered the distance in no great time, and they wondered at the size of the enemy encampment.

"God help us outsmart them, because we won't overpower them," Justus admitted.

"Outwit them we must," enjoined Lord Aelle. "No other option presents itself."

The rest of the men remained in silent awe of the sprawling encampment, thousands of men strong. The enemy tents spread out like a canvas sea in front of them, gnawing away at the hope to which they clung. The tents could be found dotted on the front of the tor, clustering more thickly toward

135

the base and spilling out into the plain. Atop the tor stood the tent of Prince Broga. Justus could see a large, black standard, emblazoned with a red dragon, snapping in the breeze in the prince's camp. A man sat astride a horse near the banner, surveying the field of battle. Justus knew that this man was Prince Broga, readying himself for the quickly approaching meeting.

The men rode slowly around the empty battlefield, biding their time and trying in vain to discover any advantage that they could before their rapidly approaching meeting with the Black Prince. Finally, the time had come, and they could see Prince Broga and his retinue ride down the tor to meet them. As he approached, Justus descried a look of disdain and animosity on the usurper's face, a dire portent of the parley to come.

"I see you have come to treat with me," began Prince Broga, upon his arrival. "'Twould be for the best if you did come hither to swear fealty to me and secure your place in my good favor."

"Would that my sword could secure its place in your pate!" shouted Lord Aelle in anger.

Prince Broga responded with an arrogant smile, feeling sure of himself with his vast army at his back.

"Lord prince," began Justus, ignoring Lord Aelle's anger, "we would see the king restored to his throne. We fight to make sure this happens. Are you willing to release King Geraint and restore him to his throne, avoiding unnecessary spilling of blood?"

"Then we fight for the same purpose, save the name of the king. I too seek to restore the true king to his crown. 'Tis mine by right and any who stand opposed," his voice rising to a crescendo, "their blood shall freely flow, their lives a fitting gift to their new king!"

Almost before Prince Broga had finished the sentence, a cry of rage came from the group of knights behind Justus. He turned in time to see a knight spurring his horse toward the prince, flailing a sword.

"Stop him!" yelled Justus, desperately hoping to avoid murder at the parley.

The knight came crashing on, nearing the prince's entourage, his sword flashing in the bright sunlight. Prince Broga's party, not suspecting treachery, was slow to react, his life only saved by his enemies. A quick thinking young knight from Justus' party quickly pulled out a bow and sent an arrow singing through the air. Lodging square in the assailants back, the arrow propelled the knight forward in the saddle, causing the assailant's swinging sword to miss its mark. The knight's horse veered to the left, avoiding the line of enemy knights, and its rider slumped from the saddle, falling at the foot of Prince Broga's horse.

"Unmask this rogue of a knight," ordered the Prince. One of his men alighted from his horse immediately, unstrapped the dead knight's helm and revealed the face of Lord Edan.

"A thousand curses upon your head," Lord Aelle spoke out sadly to the slain lord. "Your foolishness has been your undoing."

Justus rode a few paces forward to address the prince, "This man acted of his own accord, prince. Our intentions were to meet peacefully with you."

"I care not of your intentions. I have suffered an attack on my person and do deem it an act of war. As such, my knights shall strip this fool of his armor - the first spoils of battle."

Several of Prince Broga's knights joined the one already on the ground. It was only then that Justus noticed Sir Logan in Prince Broga's retinue. The fair-haired knight, his former friend, was now stripping an ally of his war gear. Justus' heart ached afresh at the treachery that Sir Logan represented.

It took but a few moments for the knights to strip the fallen lord. His work being done, Sir Logan looked up, and his gaze fell upon Justus. Sir Logan was clearly surprised to see his old friend. This was the first he knew anything of Justus' fate. Although his face could not hide his surprise, he held Justus' gaze confidently. Justus, however, awkwardly turned his gaze away in anger.

When his knights returned to their steeds, Prince Broga again spoke, "Your treachery has soured mine appetite for talk. Get you hence, doomed lords, and be prepared on the morrow for your end." He turned his horse and spurred it across the field and up the tor, his men following close behind.

Justus, Lord Aelle, and the rest likewise turned and rode back to camp in silence. Upon arrival, the lords met briefly for another council.

"Curse that insolent Lord Edan!" Lord Conall raged. "We are fortunate his was the only death this day."

"True, but it doesn't seem like much has changed," Justus interjected. "And, on the positive side, it appears like we have some more time to draw up plans for the battle tomorrow. I don't see that a delay hurts us."

"What do you think about this battle on the morrow?" added Lord Aelle, focusing the subject.

"We're at such a great disadvantage with numbers, I don't know exactly what the answer is. What I do know is that it will do us no good to charge up the hill and get slaughtered. We need to draw them onto a level playing field, if we can. If they won't meet us on the field, then we can just wait. Time is no disadvantage to us right now."

In principle, the fellow lords agreed with Justus' assertions, but they continued to deliberate for several more hours on all possible contingencies they could foresee. They might have even continued on longer, had not a messenger entered the camp, asking to speak only to Lord Justus.

"The message I bear is for none but the Lord Justus. You can impel me to tell my message to none other!" the firm voice of the messenger carried to Justus' ears as he left the deliberations to greet the messenger.

"I am Lord Justus. What message do you have for me?"

"My lord, I would speak to you in private. You can search me for weapons; I mean no treachery."

Justus agreed, and the messenger was duly searched and found with no weapons. He was welcomed into Justus' tent to disclose the contents of his message.

"Lord Justus, I am come at the behest of Sir Logan."

Justus bristled, drawing himself up to his full height in anger at the mention of the traitor's name.

"Lord, please hear what I have to say. Not is all as it seems. Sir Logan would desire to speak with you this night outside of your camp. Take what precautions you think prudent, but he must needs impart some message to you. He desires to meet with you after sundown at the edge of the wood facing away from the Tor. Whoever you bring, he wants to speak to none but you."

Justus sent the servant outside the wait, while he conferred with his fellow lords. After some short debate, it was agreed that Justus should meet with Sir Logan, although they decided he should bring an armed escort along.

Justus passed the few remaining hours vacillating between nervous anticipation and anger. He could not imagine what message his former friend and betrayer of their lord could be bringing and could foresee little else other than more treachery. But time bore on, and Justus found himself facing the reality of the meeting, rather than just its prospect. As the sun set, Justus' purposeless pacing turned to purposeful steps toward the edge of the wood, with a dozen armed men in tow.

Justus immediately stopped short when he spied the form of a man amongst the trees. The anger flared again, and Justus could feel hatred start to seep into his spirit. He came to this meeting armed and would find no scruple acquainting the traitor with his sword, should he find sufficient reason to do so. He focused his thoughts on the task at hand, away from his emotional rawness, and proceeded toward the dark figure.

As Justus came near, the figure spoke out in a harsh whisper, "My lord, keep your men at some small distance. What message I bear is to be heard by you first."

Justus didn't come this far to back out of the meeting, so he held his hand out, signaling the men to stop. Justus closed the remaining distance to the man, desiring a conclusion to the unwanted business.

"Lord," came Sir Logan's voice softly, "I know you think me a traitor of the meanest sort..."

"You are worse than that," Justus interrupted.

"Please, my lord, allow me to finish. Appearances are oft deceiving, and I beg you, allow me to restore the trust that has been lost."

Justus stood in angry silence. Sir Logan understood the silence as assent to proceed, "I was faithful to Lord Alden. I loved him, and I loved you. I love you still. 'Twas not *I* who killed our good lord. The accursed Bana was in league with Prince Broga and secured the murder of Lord Alden."

"I heard Lord Alden and Sir Bana talking about a traitor in the camp, but it was you they were talking about," retorted Justus.

"By my troth, 'twas not I who betrayed our lord..."

"You went out riding the night before. You were the only one who left. Where did you go?"

"My lord, my goodly parents died when I was but young and were laid in the earth not a league from Lord Alden's hall. Upon a successful return from battle, 'tis a habit of mine to pay my respects to their graves. That is where I rode that night. I rode to no treachery." Justus' silence compelled him to continue.

"Sir Bana was a black-hearted knave. I am sure that he aligned himself with the Black Prince and plotted the death of Lord Alden. When I returned from exercising mine horse that fateful day, I found the hall engulfed in flames and our lord in mortal combat with the treacherous Bana. Alas, but I came at the end, to find them in the midst of their final blows, felling each other, lord and traitor dead side by side. Lord Scand and his minions had routed the stronghold and none left but me to defend. I had yet avoided notice and made good my escape."

"If that's true, then why are you with Prince Broga?" Justus retorted.

"A just question, lord. 'Tis better to meet your enemy at the hearth than upon the battlefield. Were I to run to another lord, just another knight would I be against the coming black tide. Were I to convince the Black Prince that I was loyal to his cause, the damage I could do greatly increases." After a short pause, Sir Logan continued. "That is why I speak with you this night. A plan I present to you that may bring about victory this day and end the reign of the Black Prince."

"What do you have in mind?" asked Justus skeptically.

"This night, the prince and his men will drink and be merry before their expected victory on the morrow. Bring with you a small force of your best nights, scale the back of the tor, and attack the prince's camp. In the confusion, the rest of your men can attack, hopefully routing the remaining forces. For my part, I will ensure that Prince Broga will be unable to lead his men against you."

"How do I know that I can trust what you're telling me?"

"Think you back to your days of training. You did know me well. I loved you and our lord. I was faithful to the king. Faithful to the king I am still.

You do not stand to lose much. If this be a trap, then the hour of your death changes but little, for that is surely the outcome in pitched battle on the morrow."

"I will consult with the lords, but I can't make any promises right now about whether we'll be there or not." Justus did his best to seem skeptical of the idea, but the words of Lady Draic returned to his mind. Any chance to unseat Prince Broga before any black magic could be completed would make him feel better.

"No!" interjected Sir Logan. He softened quickly, "I must know before you depart. If I play my part in this scheme and you do not, I am lost. If you do not agree, then I dare not act. I *must* know."

The gravity of Sir Logan's request was obvious. Justus thought for a moment and could see no reason for the request if he was in league with the Black Prince. The enemy would not require certainty to prepare a trap. However, Sir Logan acting alone against the Prince would require certain knowledge of cooperation.

Justus made his decision and re-engaged with Sir Logan, "We will be there. Do *not* let us down."

Palpable relief showed on Sir Logan's face, "This is our only chance. My life will be sold dearly for my king if I should fail."

The discussion ended, and Sir Logan quietly made his way back to Prince Broga's camp, deftly avoiding the detection of his absence. Justus, too, returned to his camp and announced the new plan. The lords were rightly skeptical at first, but none could disavow that this might be their only chance at success. The lords departed with a prayer of success on their lips as they sought rest before the plan was to be put into action.

* * *

Several hours later, Justus set out with a group of knights and scaled the back of the Tor, as agreed with Sir Logan. The other loyal lords laid in wait for the agreed upon signal, which was the torching of the Black Prince's camp. When this was accomplished, the loyal forces would set upon the enemy in the midst of the night, hoping to God that the enemy would be defeated.

Silently, Justus found the same boulders that had hidden him before and sat with his men, observing the activity in the Prince's camp. Thus far, Sir Logan appeared to be correct. The drinking and celebrating was loud enough to drown out the sound of Justus and his men climbing the hill. The men in the camp milled about, singing songs and sloshing their drinks, laughing and making merry in the anticipation of their victory.

The raucous noise galled Justus, "I hope to end their songs shortly," he whispered to his men, who nodded in angry agreement.

Justus and his men were not the only ones put off by the celebrating. Prince Broga paced moodily by the fire, periodically glaring at the revelers in their dissipation. Not that Prince Broga disapproved of their behavior in principle, but he had too much on his mind this night to enjoy the celebration.

Finally, his frustration boiled over, "Get you to your tents and fill your gullets with ale in silence! Leave me. Now!"

The men quickly silenced their songs and headed off to their tents to continue their drinking, as Prince Broga had ordered. Only Lady Draic remained, as he had dismissed his advisors as well.

"I tell you wife, my brain does seethe with untoward thoughts this night. If only banishing them were as easy as sending revelers forth to their tents."

"What troubles you, good husband, on this, the eve of your great victory."

"Methinks that troublesome witch has despoiled my thoughts, as I cannot rid them of her prophecy."

"Do not be troubled with the ramblings of a hag. There is naught that can stand between you and your victory."

"'Tis not victory that plagues my mind, 'tis death. Did the witch not declare that I would survive an attack on my life?"

"Surely she did, my lord. What of it?"

"What of it? The attempt on my life happened this very morn! Now I have no surety for my survival, and I still know not who this landless lord is."

"Let not your thoughts plague you further. Put not words into your banfaith's mouth. She did not foretell your death but the survival of an attack."

"Forsooth she did, but my guarantee is now gone, and my thoughts are foreboding, turning again and again to death."

"Husband, you will be king on the morrow and let not fears fit only for children cause you to waver. Yet if you have concerns, why do you not increase your guard this night and enter not the fray of battle on the morrow."

"This I will do. Return you to your tent and I to mine, for fell deeds require rest."

The prince called for his advisors as Lady Draic departed. He brought them near to explain his plan, "I want double the guards 'round my tent this night, and they shall remain with me on the morrow."

His men responded immediately, calling ten more warriors to guard the prince's tent. Sir Logan accompanied his warriors to the prince, to determine which of his men would be on guard.

"Ah, Sir Logan. Fortune did bring you to me these several months, and you have discharged your duties without fail. Methinks 'twas fortune did bring you again to me this night, as I have need of you."

At this, Justus could see Sir Logan and saw him betray some visible signs of anxiety. Anxiety rose within Justus' breast as he began to consider that Prince Broga had discovered the plot and his gladness at seeing Sir Logan was in anticipation of dispensing justice.

Justus and Sir Logan did not have to wait long before being placed at ease, "I have deemed it necessary," continued Prince Broga, "to increase the guard as I sleep. Your men will be positioned around mine tent, and you will stand guard inside, guarding against treachery during my slumber."

"I am honored, my lord, to stand guard in your presence this night. I and my men shall not falter or fail." Sir Logan smiled and glanced at his men as he followed Prince Broga into his tent. The prince's advisors retired to their tents, and the guards took their places.

Justus and his men waited in anxious anticipation for some sign that they were to attack. There was no established predetermined sign from Sir Logan; Justus would have to trust that it would be obvious.

Although it felt like days to Justus, nearly an hour had passed before the first sign of anything unusual was seen. The ten warriors who Sir Logan brought with him left their posts around the tent and grouped themselves in front of the entrance. This roused the attention of the remaining guards, whose curiosity was piqued but not yet to the level of suspicion.

That all rapidly changed when a muffled cry came from the tent, followed by a wild eyed Sir Logan, who came charging out screaming, "To arms those faithful to the true king! The pretender is dead! The Black Prince is dead! To arms!"

That was the signal that Justus was looking for. He and his hidden men charged the encampment like raging bulls. At Sir Logan's cries, his ten warriors suddenly turned upon the others surrounding the tent, overwhelming them quickly. Any opposition atop the tor was soon dispatched, the sword or confused flight being the only options for those who were in Prince Broga's service.

Justus and several of his warriors touched a firebrand to the remaining flames in the fire pit and threw the fiery torches as high as they could. The flames, like a beacon in the night, alerted their waiting forces to their success. Lord Aelle and his allies poured on to the battlefield, their battle cry piercing the still night air. Soon other cries joined them, but they were cries of terror.

Word of Prince Broga's death was spreading among his men as quickly as the realization that they were being overwhelmed by those loyal to the king. The prince's army was caught completely unaware and unprepared to deal with the force that was attacking them. A few lucky escaped, fleeing for their lives, but death or capture was the fate for most of the rebel army.

Justus and his men continued to hold the Tor, which was easier than he had expected, as the confusion of the enemy prevented a concerted effort to reclaim their dead prince's camp. As the enemy attempted to flee or desperately defend their lives against the onslaught, any attempts to reclaim the high ground ceased, bringing momentary respite to Justus and his men. In those few moments, Justus paused to take in the scene unfolding below him.

He could see the outlines of dark figures engaging in mortal combat, their shadows dancing eerily by the light of the many campfires still burning. The gentle light of the stars burning above stood in peaceful contrast to the bloody battle waging beneath. The tide of the battle moved like a wave, crashing on the shore, with the loyal lords moving steadily across the base of the tor and the remnants of the tattered army attempting to flee.

Justus' reverie was broken by a hand on his shoulder and a voice in his ear, "Come, lord, let us do what we may to aid our cause. There are none left to threaten us here."

Justus turned and looked at Sir Logan and, for the first time since their separation, saw him as the friend he had once known. Whatever hostility had passed between them was now gone, and Justus was sure of his fidelity.

"I quite agree," Justus smiled. "Brave knights, descend the hill and fight your way to the closest group of allies. We will then join them and sweep the enemy away!"

The two score knights shouted their agreement and they poured down the hill as a body, yelling and hewing as they went. They joined the irresistible tide of men, sweeping away the pretender's once mighty army.

* * *

By daybreak, the fighting had ceased, and there were blessedly few casualties among the loyal lords and their men. Although victory had been gained, there was no time yet for celebration. The bodies were searched for plunder and the dead were counted, both loyal and rebel, with special attention for nobles. The prince and his closest advisors were all accounted for, Justus, Sir Logan, and their knights having done their grim work well.

In fact, there were only two bodies for which accountability eluded them – King Geraint and Lady Draic. Justus quickly ordered an expanded search of the surrounding area and in under an hour received news of the king. He had been found less than a mile away in a small enemy camp, being held apart from the battlefield to avoid rescue or his accidental death before Prince Broga could gloat in his victory. However, when word of Prince Broga's death and the routing of his army reached the camp, the soldiers quickly fled, leaving the king to the mercy of the elements.

Although haggard and ill-used in his captivity, King Geraint was in general good health. Attendants quickly descended upon him, bathing him, giving him the best food and drink available, and allowing him some repose as his army continued their work.

After spending the rest of the morning and much of the afternoon among the dead, it was determined that less than one in ten of the enemy had escaped death or capture. The rebels had been decimated and their threat destroyed. However, the body of Lady Draic was never found, nor was any book found by Justus. The surrounding areas were searched again but to no avail.

The soldiers finally quit their work and broke for nourishment, eagerly awaiting dinner, feeling famished from hours of battle and its aftermath. As hungry as the men were, they were even more anxious to see their king. Their wish was to be granted at nightfall, as the king sent word through the ranks that they were to gather for a good word from him, praising their efforts at freeing the land from impending oppression.

Justus ate his meal quickly and headed to his tent to get a short rest before the king spoke. He quickly fell into a deep, dreamless sleep and was somewhat annoyed at the interruption when he felt someone shaking his shoulder to wake him up.

"Sir," came a voice that seemed from the distant past, "as you requested, I have come to awaken you. It is eight o'clock."

Even though he had opened his eyes, it took several minutes for Justus to shake off the mental fog and realize that it was Clive who had just awakened him.

17

The End

Justus jumped up as if in a fright. "It's her. I know it is! We've got to go. Now!"

"Pardon me, sir, but may I ask what is the cause for your agitation?"

"Clive, I think I've put it together, and we're running out of time. I have to try this as soon as possible. I'll explain on the way."

Justus grabbed some flashlights and darted out of the house, across the fields, and through the woods to reach the descent into the ravine. Clive was struggling to keep up, but Justus did not seem to notice in his preoccupied state.

"Sir, I have got to take a rest," Clive yelled ahead to Justus. "If I don't catch my breath, I don't believe I'll be able to make the descent safely. In the meantime, you might explain the situation to me."

Justus was glad for the quick breather and, after a few deep breaths, began to explain, "Clive, I had another dream last night. I saw her again, the woman in the tomb, Lady Draic. She was the wife of a usurping prince named Broga. It's weird, because each night's dream seems to build on the last one, and last night seemed to be the climax. I was leading a vastly undermanned army against Prince Broga's forces. We ended up defeating his army, but his wife escaped, and we never could find her.

"I don't know if my dreams represent some sort of history or not, but

Lady Draic was real. I can't prove any of this, but the sicker Anna has gotten, the more alive this woman looks in her tomb. I fear that somehow she has preserved herself until some unsuspecting person finds the book and starts to read it. Somehow this must trigger whatever sorcery has been placed on that book. From what I've heard in my dream and what's happening now, reading the book has caused one person's vitality to be transferred into another. I thought it would have been the reader, but for some reason Anna's life is slowly drained from her until her death, which reanimates Lady Draic. I believe she's stealing Anna's life away, while I get pulled back to Lady Draic's time. I overheard her discussing it, and it seems like this is a side effect of the magic she didn't anticipate."

"What do you propose to do?"

"Let's not waste any more time standing up here. You'll find out very shortly."

They descended the gorge as quickly as safety would allow. The beauty of the surroundings that had struck Justus previously was now lost on him, as he leaped across stream and stone on his mad dash to the cave opening. Clive followed as closely as he could manage, arriving a few moments after Justus. He stood panting, needing another respite before proceeding into the mouth of the cave.

Justus headed inside before Clive was quite recovered, but his butler dutifully followed close behind. Like a moth drawn to a flame, Justus purposefully strode toward the terminal end of the cave, where the burial chamber was. In a few moments, they arrived at their destination.

Up until the instant Justus entered the chamber, he was completely confident of his mission. However, doubt began to creep into his mind. What if his idea didn't work? What if his theory of what was going on was completely wrong, and he had wasted precious time away from his dying wife? The doubt began to paralyze him as he stood rooted to the floor just inside the chamber. It was Clive who snapped him out of his trance.

"Sir, ought we not remove the lid?" using the gentlest way to get Justus moving that he could find.

"What if it doesn't work, Clive? I mean, what if I'm all wrong?"

"Then there is nothing anyone could do. Fanciful or not, you are pursuing the only plausible way you know to help your wife. There does not seem to be much to lose by trying."

"You're right. Let's get this lid off and see what we're dealing with."

The two men slowly lifted the lid and laid it next to the sarcophagus. Perspiration stood out on Justus' forehead as he set the lid down, due more to the anxiety of what he would find in the casket than from the actual exertion of lifting the lid. He righted himself and paused for a brief moment before looking in at the body. When he did, he caught his breath.

The woman in the sarcophagus was beautiful and whole. Justus recognized her instantly as Lady Draic. Her metamorphosis from a dried out husk to a full-fleshed, life-like woman was complete. She was a stunning vision of a woman asleep on the verge of waking up. Her soft expression as she teetered on the brink of death and life stood in stark contrast to the wickedness of her spirit. Her beauty and innocent face almost made Justus feel repentant for what he had made his mind up to do. Looking so life-like also gave him pause. He was not a murderer and did not like how alive she looked.

Justus steeled his nerves and repeated to himself several times that she was, in fact, still dead and that his precious wife's life was on the line. He would do just about anything for his Anna, and he knew this needed to be done. Stepping forward, Justus laid hold of the sword at the woman's breast and lifted it away from her. Clive immediately divined what Justus meant to do and stepped away. His sense of propriety would not allow him to watch the deed itself.

Clutching the hilt, Justus raised the sword, blade poised above the dragon emblazoned on her breast. He closed his eyes shut tight against the ghastly deed about to be done. A moment's pause passed while he gathered his courage. A shout, meant as much to distract as to strengthen, escaped Justus' lips as he thrust the sword down. Much to his relief, there was no accompanying shout from the body, no convulsions or death rattles. A small trickle of blood escaped from the corner of her mouth, leaving a crimson trail down her pale cheek.

Justus stepped back, only to realize that he hadn't considered what to do with the sword. He had left it protruding from the body. He felt like it was improper to leave it there but was loathe to step up and remove it. Fortunately, he was spared the decision. As he looked on, the body began to reverse the metamorphosis it had undertaken. The life-likeness seemed to drain from the body. The fat and muscle began to wither, and the skin began to parch and shrivel. In the matter of a few short moments, the body had returned to its original state of skin stretched over bone. However, the body was no longer held in the stasis that kept it from its final decay. Soon there was nothing left but dust to receive the falling sword as the body that held it in place turned to ash. The sword clanked against the stone, giving finality to the situation and snapping Justus out of his trance.

"I think we've done it, Clive," breathed Justus visibly relieved to have the deed done. "I guess I didn't really know what would happen, but it looks like whatever was keeping her from decomposing has been broken."

"That is an encouraging sign, sir. We may be best served to see if it had the desired result."

"You're absolutely right. Here I am standing like a dolt when Anna's life is in the balance. Let's get going," said Justus, concluding the conversation even as he ran from the chamber.

This time, Justus didn't wait for Clive. He sprinted toward the cave mouth, barely pausing for his eyes to adjust before he began scaling the ravine like a pack of wolves were on his tail. He cleared the rim of the gorge and sped on his way toward his house. It wasn't until he barged through the front door that he thought to look back for Clive. His impatience peaked when he saw Clive seeming to struggle over the rim.

Justus perhaps was prepared to make a bigger show of his impatience when Clive arrived until he perceived the reason for Clive's slowness. As the man neared the house, it became clear that he was carrying a burden. This burden soon revealed itself to be the sword from the burial chamber. Interest quickly overcame his impatience as Clive reached the house.

"Why did you bring the sword?" Justus queried as they ran to the car.

"Sir, in the dreams you've been having, it appears you have learned the value of a sword and used a sword to bring about victory. If you are right, and your wife returns to health, then I should think you would want it to commemorate this victory."

Justus was amazed at the foresight of his butler and hoped he was right. If Anna died, then the sword would be sorry consolation. However, if Anna was restored to health, the sword would commemorate the preciousness of his wife's life and those he came to know and love in his dreams. Even if they were just dreams, they helped shape his life and his fight for his wife's.

Silence and anxiety reigned during the drive to the hospital. Justus was sure his heart would burst out of his chest with anxious anticipation. The miles seemed to drag on and the minutes felt like hours until they finally pulled onto hospital grounds.

The car had hardly stopped before Justus fairly leaped from the car and sprinted toward the hospital entrance. His stride barely faltered even as he entered the building. Several other people entered the elevator with him, as he quickly pressed the button for the fifth floor. He was horrified to see the buttons light up for the second, third, and fourth floor, as fellow riders departed at each floor before his stop. Justus could only look disconsolately at Clive until the elevator doors finally opened to reveal the fifth floor. He ran to Anna's room, but abruptly stopped short, almost causing Clive to run into him.

"What is it sir?" asked Clive, quickly recovering from the near collision.

"What if she's dead, Clive? I guess I've been avoiding the thought until now. But I could be just several feet away from finding out that the love of my life is gone forever. I'm afraid."

"Of course you are, and no one could fault you for it. But keep a stiff upper lip, sir. There could be something other than death waiting for you in that room." Justus closed his eyes and silently sent up a prayer of supplication before entering the room.

As he entered, his knees almost buckled, and his vision blurred from the tears welling in his eyes. The sight that greeted him was the pale, motionless figure of his wife in the hospital bed. Justus leaned on the door for support, fighting vainly to suppress the welling grief and disappointment at his failure. He was surprised at the facility with which Clive approached his wife's deathbed.

"Pardon me, you are Anna's husband, correct?" came a voice owned by a man in a white lab coat by the bed.

"Yes…Yes…," was all he could utter.

"Well, we are very pleased with your wife's progress this morning. She seems to be recovering very quickly; I am not even sure why. Her vital signs are stable, and she's resting comfortably."

"You mean…," Justus paused before uttering the words of hope, "she's alive?"

"To be sure. She's quite alive. She will need to stay with us a few days to be monitored and to help her recover her strength, but right now we see absolutely no signs of illness."

Justus' knees nearly buckled again. To have hope return so forcefully after he had lost it was almost more than his system could take. Recovering his poise, he quickly gained his wife's bedside and grasped her hand. He knelt down beside the bed, pressing his cheek to her hand and let the tears of joy flow. After a moment, the hand moved from his cheek, stroking it lightly, before finding its way back into his hands. Justus quickly stood up and looked into Anna's eyes. Tears began to flow again when he recognized the familiar spark of life in her eyes, though somewhat dulled from her ordeal.

Justus spent the remainder of the day at his wife's side as she slept. He gloried in her deep, even breathing, thinking that he had never seen anything so beautiful as the gentle rise and fall of Anna's chest. Breathing meant life; Anna was alive. He had to keep reminding himself in order for it to seem real.

Clive had left for the house hours before to continue his duties at Ascalon Cottage. However, as evening gave way to night, Clive returned to take Justus home. The emotional ordeal of the day had exhausted him, and he went straight to the bedroom and fell asleep, forgoing the supper that Clive had prepared.

* * *

Justus awoke from his peaceful, blessedly dreamless sleep as sunlight poured through the bedroom window. A flood of relief passed over him as he remembered the events of the previous day. But before he could fully enjoy the moment, a terrible thought crept into his head – he hadn't read the book last night. Would that omission impact his wife's recovery? She took a sudden turn for the worse the last time he hadn't read the book. He hurriedly dressed, alerting Clive to his departure, virtually sprinting to the car while doing so.

The reality of her recovery finally set in, dashing all lingering doubts, when Justus found Anna sitting up in her hospital bed, chatting amicably with a nurse. He ran to Anna and embraced her. Even as he held her thin frame, he consoled himself with the hope that she would quickly return to her old self.

"Hi honey," Anna said, greeting Justus cheerfully. "I feel so much better, especially now that you're here."

"I thought I'd lost you. I thought I'd lost you," was all Justus could say in that moment, tears welling up in his eyes again.

"I don't give up that easily, but I have to admit that I was scared too. Thankfully the doctors think it's all behind me. They're going to run some tests on me pretty soon here, just to make sure everything looks normal. That will take most of the morning, and I'll be resting much of the afternoon, but the doctors think I can come home tomorrow if everything looks good."

A beatific smile beamed from his face at his wife's encouraging words. He spent the next hour or so at Anna's side until the doctors needed her for the tests. He was reluctant to go, but she was adamant.

"Honey, go home and take care of yourself. Waiting here for hours as they are running tests won't do anyone any good. Plus, I'll be resting this evening. The doctors want me to be as rested as possible for tomorrow morning. And I want *you* to be as rested as possible for tomorrow, too."

He bent over and kissed her gently on the forehead. He clasped her hand until the nurses came for her. He released her, sad to be going, but alive with the prospect of having his wife back home with him.

He soaked in his happiness like the sunshine pouring through the car windows as he drove back to Ascalon cottage. Tears of joy moistened his eyes several times on the trip, but he was able to compose himself as he arrived home.

Clive came to greet Justus at the door and welcomed the wonderful news. Their arrival set Clive into a flurry of activity to ensure everything was as it should be for the return of the mistress of the house. The sudden departure of Clive into the depths of their home allowed other thoughts to crowd into Justus' brain. The foremost was his fear from this morning that he hadn't read last night. It seemed to him like it had been years since the last time he hadn't read the book before going to sleep, so he entered the library to find the source of his early morning anxiety.

Much to his surprise, the book was gone. Its location was marked by an empty space on the bookshelf. Justus mounted the ladder to take a closer look and only found a small pile of dust where the book should have been. He stepped down and looked around the library for it. Even as he was searching, he knew it was a mere formality and that he would never find the book again. Nevertheless, the exercise of looking for it was gratifying, further solidifying his confidence in his wife's recovery.

During the search, he was surprised to notice something on the table in the center of the room that he had not noticed when he entered the library, his attention being fixed on thoughts of the book. Inside a beautiful mahogany case, glassed about the sides and top, was the sword from the cave. The piece looked exquisite in the room and seemed to be a perfect compliment to the décor. Justus immediately set out to find Clive.

"Clive, when did you get that case for the sword? It looks beautiful."

"Even as I was carrying it up the side of the ravine, I was thinking what to do with it, and I've been working the last several days to procure it. Upon the news of improvement, I took the liberty of purchasing it and setting it up in the library. Sir, it is an appropriate symbol of conquest, placed in the most appropriate location. It shall always be a reminder of how you redeemed your wife's life."

"How *we* did, you mean. I couldn't have done it without you. I love it in there. Thank you so much." Justus augmented his words with an affectionate grasping of Clive's closest shoulder with his hand. With an appreciative nod of his head, Clive continued his preparations for Anna's happy return.

As with all things, no matter how long they seem in the coming, the time for waiting drew to a close. Justus had slept soundly in those moments that his blissful anticipation would allow him, and he was up with the sunshine, readying himself for what he hoped was the final trip to the hospital. Much to his relief, the phone rang, with Anna's merry voice on the other end, confirming her release that morning.

If he thought he couldn't go any faster, hearing Anna's voice compelled him on even more. He raced to the hospital and waited impatiently while the discharge was finalized and a follow-up appointment was made to ensure progress.

The overwhelming emotion felt by the happy couple on the way home precluded any conversation. They sat hand-in-hand reveling in each other's blessed company. It wasn't until they were pulling down the lane toward Ascalon Cottage before Anna's thoughts began to turn toward her cherished home.

"I can't wait to get home. I never really had a chance to enjoy the house before I got sick. I feel like I'm really coming home for the first time."

"I'm glad we'll finally enjoy it together. We were both excited about so many things, and it was hollow without you. You never actually did get to enjoy the library much that we were so looking forward to."

"I know, I was *just* thinking about the library. I'm feeling well enough today that I won't need to rest right away when we get in. Let's go right to the library and start enjoying it together like we wanted to."

Justus pulled to a stop in the circular driveway in front of the cottage and gratefully helped his wife out of the car. Clive was standing at the door and greeted her as enthusiastically as his sense of propriety would allow. Anna gave him a warm embrace and entered into her home, feeling as if she were seeing it with new eyes. She laid hold of Justus' hand, bringing him quickly into the library. She plopped down on the couch, luxuriating in the fascinating library and was about to prop up her feet when she noticed the sword on the table.

"Honey, where did you get that sword? It's beautiful."

"Now *that,* my love," Justus said through a suppressed smile, "is a long story."

www.ingramcontent.com/pod-product-compliance
Lightning Source LLC
Chambersburg PA
CBHW060457300726

48975CB00008B/2539